"I understand, B...

He turned around, his face still contorted by anger. "You understand *what*?"

"Why you're so mad at me," Cassie said. "I would be, too."

He shook his head. "It's not just you I'm mad at. I never should have blown up at you like that. I feel like I'm losing control. Reverting back to who I used to be."

"I should have told you about the trafficking ring. But the timing still doesn't work for them to have grabbed Ashley here."

"But even the slightest chance…"

"If you'll let me, I'd still like to help you find her. Work together on our cases."

"I can't do it unless you're going to be completely honest with me. About everything."

"Fine. But that goes for you, too."

"Deal. But don't tell me what I legally can and can't do."

"All right. But don't ask me to do anything illegal. Or unethical. Or—"

"Okay, okay." His mouth kicked up at the corners. "When do we start?"

RESOLUTE JUSTICE

—

LESLIE MARSHMAN

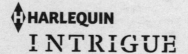

For Ann.

Thank you for the late-night calls to check on my sanity,

and your invaluable feedback that made this a stronger book.

Am I approaching the innermost circle yet?

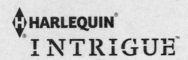

HARLEQUIN®

INTRIGUE™

Recycling programs for this product may not exist in your area.

ISBN-13: 978-1-335-55562-5

Resolute Justice

Copyright © 2022 by Leslie Marshman

This edition published by arrangement with Harlequin Books S.A.

For questions and comments about the quality of this book, please contact us at CustomerService@Harlequin.com.

Harlequin Enterprises ULC
22 Adelaide St. West, 41st Floor
Toronto, Ontario M5H 4E3, Canada
www.Harlequin.com

Printed in U.S.A.

Multi-award-winning author **Leslie Marshman** writes novels featuring strong heroines, the heroes who love them and the bad guys who fear them. She called Denver home until she married a Texan without reading the fine print. Now she lives halfway between Houston and Galveston and embraces the humidity. When Leslie's not writing, you might find her camping at a lake, fishing pole in one hand and a book in the other. Visit her at www.lesliemarshman.com, www.Facebook.com/lesliemarshmanauthor, www.Instagram.com/leslie_marshman or @lesliemarshman on Twitter.

Books by Leslie Marshman

Harlequin Intrigue

Resolute Justice

Visit the Author Profile page at Harlequin.com.

CAST OF CHARACTERS

Cassie Reed—Acting Boone County sheriff since her father, the previous sheriff, was killed on duty. A stickler for following the letter of the law, she's after a human-trafficking ring as well as her father's killers. But someone keeps tipping off the bad guys.

Tyler "Bishop" Bishop—Previously a reputable detective with the Houston Police Department, he's now a laid-back private investigator, practicing yoga and meditation to manage his stress. His search for his missing eighteen-year-old niece/goddaughter brings him to Resolute.

Adam Reed—Eldest of the Reed brothers, he's one of Cassie's six deputies. But someone is trying to frame him and Noah as the source of the leaks.

Noah Reed—He and his twin, Nate, are the youngest Reeds. He's also one of his sister's deputies.

Nate Reed—The only Reed not a member of the sheriff's department, he came home for his father's funeral after several years of traveling and trying to find himself.

Lonnie Dixon—Cousin to the Reed siblings and a longtime deputy, he's now chief deputy as well as Cassie's trusted right-hand man.

Dave Sanders—The last deputy to join the department, he harbors a grudge toward Noah.

Chapter One

A jagged thread of excitement ripped through Sheriff Cassie Reed's chest as she tugged the Velcro strap. Tightening the Kevlar vest against her ribs, she felt along the sides, confirming there were no gaps.

This was her first raid since being appointed Boone County sheriff. She and her deputies worked quickly, speaking in whispers. They'd parked around the corner, out of sight from the small house that was their target.

Cassie's younger brother Noah approached her. "You sure you don't want me at the back door with Lonnie and Adam?" Noah, like Cassie and their brother Adam, had followed their father into law enforcement. Only Nate, Noah's twin, had yet to decide what he wanted to do with his life.

"Your vest is buckling. Turn around." Cassie reached up and adjusted the straps on his broad shoulders. Then she patted the back pocket of the Kevlar encasing Noah's muscular frame, huffing her annoyance. "Where's your rear trauma pad?"

He fidgeted beneath the body armor. "It's too freaking hot."

Anger laced with fear shot through Cassie, and she spun him around to face her. Gripping his shoulders, she looked up into brown eyes the same warm hue as their father's. "It's never too hot to die. Dagnabbit, Noah, you know better."

Noah's enthusiasm for the job still exceeded his experience. And truthfully, after everything that had happened over the past few months, she was usually glad for that. There were days when the gleam in her brother's eyes and his winning rookie smile helped hold back the pain of so recently losing their dad. But she would take no chances where his safety was concerned. And that went for everyone on her team.

"By the book, Deputy."

"Yeah, yeah. But what about the back door?"

"We're going according to plan. You're with me at the front." She ignored Noah's muttered curse and added, "Get the pad in that pocket. We're ready to roll."

Cassie gave the go signal to Chief Deputy Lonnie Dixon. Though not yet forty, Lonnie's once lean and trim physique had softened, and his dark beard boasted more than a few gray hairs. But he could still bring down a fugitive who had a decent head start. He'd become Cassie's indispensable right-hand man since she'd assumed the job of sheriff.

At her signal, Lonnie led half the men down the

dirt alley that bisected the block. From there, they'd get into position behind the detached one-car garage and the backyard storage shed, staying hidden from the security camera at the rear of the house.

Using large oak trees in neighboring yards as cover, Cassie and her group leapfrogged toward the front. They knew from earlier surveillance that the window curtains along both sides of the house never moved. But the camera near the front door would announce their presence as soon as they crossed the property line.

Cassie pressed the button on her mic. "Approaching door now. Get ready."

"Ten-four." Lonnie's voice came back in a whisper.

She and Noah ran up the front steps and to the left of the door. Longtime deputy Sean Cavanaugh's powerful biceps bulged as he carried the breacher to the right side.

Cassie leaned forward just far enough to knock, then bellowed, "Sheriff's Department! We have a warrant to search the premises. Open up!"

No response. She checked her watch. After waiting the required number of seconds, she reached for the knob. Locked. She backed away and nodded at Sean, speaking into her mic. "Breaching."

"In position." Lonnie's calm voice assured her they were ready in the back.

As the battering ram hit the door, it splintered like dried kindling. Cassie entered in a crouch, swinging her gun toward the living room on the left. Noah followed, covering the small room to the right.

Sean dropped the ram and ran past them to the first doorway. "Bedroom. Clear."

Cassie moved down the hallway, Noah on her heels. Room by room, they confirmed the house was vacant. Sean unlocked the back door, letting Lonnie, Adam and Deputy Peter Grant into the cramped, trash-filled kitchen.

"They're not here?" Lonnie's tone gave shape to the disappointment cramping Cassie's gut. *Not again.* She'd been sure this time. Done everything by the book. Taken no chances on a leak that could have warned them off.

"Nope." She bit off the word, then blew out a breath of frustration. "But they were." Eyes sweeping across her men, she issued orders. "Listen up, everybody. Gloves on. Touch nothing. If you see something that's potential evidence, set down a marker and call Brett. He's the investigator Travis County sent us, and he's our finder today."

She pressed her mic and called in Brett Miller, the forensic technician waiting back at the vehicles, then continued with her commands. "Pete, Noah, bedrooms. Sean, the front two rooms. Lonnie, you take the garage and shed." She glanced at Adam. "Sorry, bro. That leaves the kitchen and bathroom for you."

"Hey, that's why you pay me the big bucks,

right?" Nothing ever seemed to affect his cheerful mood. Not even a sink filled with dirty dishes and putrid, scummy water she could smell from across the room.

Two years younger than Cassie, Adam had been upbeat even as a child. He'd never complained about helping her with household chores and had taken over as the family cook when Cassie's attempts at the stove proved inedible.

He tucked his slightly-too-long, dark blond hair behind his ears and rolled up his sleeves.

"How long since you've been to the barber? Your hair's almost past regulation length."

"So's yours, sis." He flipped her high ponytail, then laughed when she grabbed the end to measure by touch against her shirt. "Don't worry, it's barely hitting the top of your collar." Adam fought the August humidity to pull on a pair of nitrile gloves. "Besides, who's gonna yell at you for long hair? You're the boss now."

"I don't follow the regulations to avoid getting reprimanded." Convinced her ponytail had stayed where it should be, she let go of it. "I follow them *because* they're the regulations."

"Well, go follow them somewhere else, *boss*. I'm fixin' to be elbow-deep in this sink water. Just hope nothing's alive in there."

As her men searched their assigned areas, Cassie began her own process. She walked back to the front door, closed her eyes, and turned around. Inhaling a deep breath, she sorted through the odors that fought for her attention. Stale fried food. Unwashed bodies. The acrid scent of fear.

She opened her eyes, taking in the front rooms as if for the first time. No furniture other than a couple of card tables and some folding chairs. Internet cables and extension cords lay coiled on the floor like Mexican black kingsnakes.

A soft knock right behind her yanked Cassie's attention back to the open front door. Brett Miller stood on the sill holding his crime scene case, ID clipped to his pocket. She waved her hand for him to follow her into the living room, stepping over pizza boxes and empty beer cans, porn magazines and used condoms.

"I want every single thing in this house bagged." Cassie glanced at the CSI, a young man she hadn't worked with before.

Brett rubbed the back of his neck, his gaze sweeping across the trash-covered carpeting. "You don't think it's just kids using this as a party house?"

Cassie tipped her head to the side, peering at him. "You been working crime scenes long, Brett?"

A red flush crept up his cheeks. "No, ma'am. This is my first solo case."

Cassie pursed her lips and nodded. "Follow me." She led him into a bedroom. "Tell me what you see."

"Some pretty disgusting mattresses."

"Anything else?"

"More trash." Brett shrugged. "I mean, it looks like some kids had a sex fest. Ma'am."

Cassie pointed to where the wall and ceiling met near the door. "See the damaged drywall up there? That happens when security or video cameras are ripped out in a hurry." She tapped the toe of her well-worn cowboy boot on a large metal eyebolt screwed into the floor. There were two bolts by each mattress. Four filthy mattresses in each of the three bedrooms. "Now, I've never been to a sex fest myself, but I doubt that cuffing girls to the floor puts them in a festive mood."

The color drained from Brett's face. "I didn't realize—"

"Garage is clear." Lonnie's deep voice interrupted them. He stood in the doorway, his lip curled with disgust as he eyed the wall-to-wall stained mattresses.

Cassie acknowledged Lonnie by holding up one finger, then refocused on Brett. "I don't doubt you're well trained. But if you want to work my crime scenes, you need to be a lot more observant. Your job isn't jumping to conclusions and ignoring potential evidence. It's collecting every piece of garbage, every disgusting hair from the drains, every fingerprint, footprint and drop of blood. Lives are at stake, Brett."

She paused, a painful lump forming in the back of her throat. It wasn't just the lives of the faceless victims she'd sworn to protect that were endangered. The painful memory of her father's sightless eyes and bloody uniform pushed its way forward. The lives of people she loved most in the world were also at risk. "Look, I've been chasing these monsters for two years. And when we catch them, I sure as heck don't want the case thrown out because someone didn't handle evidence correctly. I'm depending on you to do your job by the book, without cutting any corners."

Brett looked down and nodded. "Yes, ma'am."

Cassie followed Lonnie to the living room, Brett tight on her heels. She cocked a questioning brow at the investigator.

"I'm gonna need more evidence bags." Brett walked through the front doorway, calling over his shoulder, "They're in my van."

"Newbie?" Lonnie asked, hooking a thumb toward Brett's retreating back.

Nodding, Cassie swiped at a trickle of sweat sliding past her eye. The late August heat had turned the small house into an oven. "Yep. But I think he got the message. I have a feeling Brett's going to turn out to be an excellent criminalist." She turned her full attention to Lonnie. "What were you saying about the garage?"

"It's empty, but there are some muddy footprints. Took some pictures. We might be able to ID the shoes."

"Great. Then all we have to do is find the man

wearing those shoes." She clenched her teeth until her jaw ached.

Lonnie shrugged. "Better than nothing."

Cassie walked down the short hall to the kitchen at the back. "What about the shed?"

"It's locked. Your brother went back to the truck to get the cutters."

Noah walked past them just then with a pair of long-handled bolt cutters resting on his shoulder. He cocked a brow toward his older sister. "I call first dibs if it's full of money."

Anger at being one step behind these scum-sucking human traffickers sharpened her tone. "This is no time to joke about your get-rich-quick schemes. The young women taken by these brutes are facing a horrible future, if they even have a future." Her brother's grin faded, and she and Lonnie followed a subdued Noah through the back door and across the yard in silence.

A quick snip through the padlock's shank and the doors swung open with a rusty squeal. A lawn mower sat center stage, yellowed newspapers covered with oil spots beneath it. Pushed up against one wall, a potting bench held remnants of broken terra-cotta planters and a tipped-over container of fire ant killer.

"Man, I hate that stuff." Noah eyed the insecticide on the bench. "Always smells like something died."

"Yeah, but it works." Lonnie eased past the

mower and around a stack of boxes. "Nothin' back here but cobwebs, dead roaches, and…"

"And what?" Cassie asked.

"And I think you're gonna want to see this."

Cassie joined Lonnie, who was bent over a blue canvas tarp. He lifted a corner with gloved fingers, revealing a body. Cassie crouched down for a closer look, but layers of clouded plastic sheeting encased the body like a mummy and obscured the features. Only escaped strands of long blond hair indicated their vic might be a female.

"Based on the smell, I'd guess she's been dead a while." Lonnie ducked his head away to inhale.

Cassie shook her head. "I don't think so. I think it's the heat in here." Her fingers itched to open the plastic, get a better look, but she couldn't risk destroying evidence.

"I thought you said that stench was the fire ant powder." Noah peered around the stacked boxes. *"Whoa."*

"Actually, you were the one who said that." Cassie glanced up at her brother's ashen face. Despite being a deputy for several years, this was Noah's first homicide. "You okay?"

He nodded like a dashboard bobblehead, apparently afraid to open his mouth in case more than just words came out.

"If you're going to get sick, get your butt back outside," Lonnie snapped. "Worst thing you can do is contaminate the scene."

"I'm not gonna get sick." Noah glared at Lonnie.

Proud of her brother's fortitude, Cassie stood and pulled her phone from her pocket. "Noah, go get Brett. And call the justice of the peace. Tell him we need a death verification ASAP." She began snapping preliminary pictures of the body and the scene.

Noah headed for the house, but his yell across the backyard carried all the way into the shed. "Brett, Cassie needs you out here. We got a body burrito."

Lonnie shook his head. "He's got a lot to learn."

"You don't have to tell me." Cassie bit her lip to hide her amusement. "But he has what it takes. It's in his DNA."

"It takes more than that."

Cassie gave him a gentle punch in the arm. "Oh, lighten up. At least he's not cranky and cynical, like a certain chief deputy I know."

Equipment box in hand, Brett jogged up to them and addressed Cassie. "Where's the body?"

"Inside, back behind the boxes. Wrapped in plastic, under the blue tarp."

"You call the JP?" The investigator was already slipping paper booties over his shoes.

Cassie nodded. "But it'll probably take him a while to get here. Usually does."

"Okay." Brett squatted next to his kit, grabbing gloves and evidence markers. "I called my office, too, told them we need a couple more techs and a transport vehicle. I'll get started with the initial walk-through out here."

Pleased that her assessment of Brett's potential seemed on point, Cassie motioned Lonnie outside. "Can you go check on the progress in the house? If they find *anything*, make sure they wait for the rest of the forensic team to get here to process it. I want to keep an eye on the body while we wait for the JP."

"You don't trust the newbie?" Lonnie kept his voice low.

"It's not that. I'm just not taking any chances this time."

Lonnie gave her a sympathetic look that irritated Cassie more than she'd ever admit. "Don't worry, boss lady. We'll get 'em."

She blew out a frustrated breath. "Two years, Lonnie. And catching these creeps is proving harder than putting socks on a rooster."

TYLER BISHOP PRESSED the doorbell, laughing out loud when Beethoven's "Für Elise" chimed inside his brother's garish Houston McMansion. Bob hadn't known Beethoven from Black Sabbath before marrying his second wife. Not that *Monique* knew anything about classical music, either. But then, what did one expect from a pretentious gold digger?

While he waited on the front porch, his gut churned like he'd overdone the hot sauce on his breakfast taco. He'd bet the ranch there was more to his brother's invitation than just being sociable. But after a two-year moratorium on visits, at least he'd get to see his niece.

Ashley had taken after her mother, Beth. Blonde, pretty and with a bubbly personality, she loved life. Well, she had until Beth's devastating fight with cancer left Ashley motherless at an age when a girl needed her mom the most.

He reached into the right pocket of his blazer, anticipating her reaction to the turtle key chain he'd brought her. Her fascination with turtles began when she was a toddler, resulting in her nickname. *Little Turtle.* He had brought her one whenever he'd seen her. So far, her favorite had been a silver turtle necklace, inset with pieces of Mexican opal. He'd given it to her four years ago, on her fourteenth birthday.

The front door swung inward, framing Monique in the opening. Her knee-length, sleeveless blue dress revealed well-toned arms and legs. *Personal trainer? Tennis pro? Pool boy?*

"Tyler." Bob's wife was a displaced Yankee, but despite her bogus Southern accent she still managed to impart resignation, disappointment and distaste in only two little syllables.

And the wrong two at that. He'd gone by Bishop since seventh grade when he and another Tyler agreed to use last names to avoid confusion. Only

Bob and his parents still called him Tyler. And now, Monique.

"Monique." Bishop matched her tone but didn't try for the exaggerated drawl.

"Come in." She stepped back, motioning him into the three-story foyer.

"Thanks." Bishop's gaze took in the sweeping staircase to the second floor, modern art on the walls and the crystal chandelier hanging far above their heads. "I gotta admit, the invitation surprised me."

Monique sighed. "Now is not the time to be petty, Tyler."

"Petty? Listen, I've respected your demands to have no contact with my brother and niece…"

"I simply don't think the lifestyle of a homeless private investigator sets a good example for an impressionable teenager. Nor does it reflect well on our family name."

Our. As if *he* was the latest addition to the family instead of her. "You know I'm not homeless, Monique."

"Well, the *house-sitting* does seem to be a permanent situation, doesn't it?" She even used freaking air quotes, just in case he missed her disparaging tone.

"Tye!" Bob's cheerful greeting didn't match the tight smile that cracked across his haggard face. His shoulders slumped and dark circles rimmed his bloodshot eyes. Bishop fought to keep his mouth from dropping open. *He looks like an old man*. Warning bells clanged. What had aged his brother since their last covert meetup for coffee a few months ago?

"Thanks for coming. I..." Bob glanced at Monique. "*We* need your help."

On high alert now, Bishop followed his brother into a formal living room that he vaguely remembered from his only other visit to the house.

Please, let it be something simple, like divorce. Just the possibility improved his mood.

He sat on an uncomfortable, overly ornate chair with asymmetrical arms while his brother dropped onto a weird-shaped couch with only half a back and a ridiculous flaring armrest. No, not a couch. A *settee*. Funny how a word you've never used can pop into your brain at the appropriate moment. Monique lowered herself gracefully next to Bob. The settee's odd form suddenly made sense. Monique needed nothing behind her. The stick up her butt kept her upright.

"You going to tell me what's going on?"

A housekeeper came to the doorway and waited, brows raised.

"Coffee?" Bob asked Bishop.

Monique inhaled a tiny gasp, and Bishop glanced at the Oriental rug beneath the glass coffee table. When someone with the legal name of Monica insisted it be pronounced *Monique*, what were the odds her furnishings were authentic? But why poke the bear?

"Better pass. I'd hate to accidentally soil your rug." Bishop leaned back in the chair and rested one ankle across the opposite knee. Bits of dried mud from the edge of his boot heel flaked onto the floor, giving him a sense of satisfaction that he had to admit was, indeed, petty.

No comeback from his brother. Instead, Bob slouched forward, elbows on knees, and rested his face in his palms. Bishop almost regretted his sarcastic reply, but it wasn't easy to get past being unfairly ostracized by the only family he had left.

Lowering his hands, Bob blurted out, "Ashley's missing, and we need your help to find her."

"What do you mean, she's missing?" Bishop dropped his foot to the floor and leaned forward. "Since when?"

"Really, it's not like she hasn't done this before." Icicles dripped from Monique's words. "Several times, in fact. She'll be back when she's done being annoyed with us."

Bishop's gaze slid from his sister-in-law to his brother. "Bob?"

Monique rose. "*Robert* can fill you in on the details. I have an appointment I must keep."

"Botox injections?" Bishop asked.

Monique narrowed her eyes at him, pivoted like a model at the end of a runway and sashayed out of the room.

Bob's sidelong glance followed her, disappointment written across his face. "It's true. Ashley *has* run away before. But in the past she always stayed at her friend Kim's house, and Kim's parents would let us know." Bob scrubbed his face with his hands. "But not this time. We haven't heard from her. We called around. No one's seen her."

"Did you contact the police?"

"The first day. But between her age and her history of running away, they shut me down. Said I should reach out to her friends and relatives." He raised red-rimmed eyes to Bishop. "Is that right? Can they really refuse to do anything?"

"Unless there's evidence that Ashley left against her will, there's not much they can do. They might take a missing persons report, but they won't actively search for her." Bishop pulled a small notebook and pen from his jacket pocket. Old habit left over from his days as an HPD detective. "When did you last see her?"

"Four days ago. Sunday." Bob blew out a hard breath. "She was upset because her boyfriend had to go back home for some sort of family emergency, and Monique wouldn't let her see him before he took off."

Bishop glanced up from his notes. "Any chance she took off with the boyfriend?"

"I guess it's possible. But we don't have his phone number, so we haven't been able to reach him. We started by calling Kim and all of Ashley's other friends. None of them have seen her. Not a one." His hands clasped together in a death grip. "Every single one of them said she hadn't even mentioned running away to them. I thought teenagers told their closest friends everything. This isn't normal, is it? For a runaway, I mean."

"You believe them?"

Bob nodded. "They're a good group of kids, for the most part."

"And the boyfriend? What's his name?"

"Michael Pugh. Nice enough kid, from what I've seen."

"So what was Monique's issue with Ashley seeing him before he left town?"

"He's a couple of years older than Ashley. He moved here from some small town near Victoria or San Antonio. Stays with an uncle here in Houston, I think. Works at Old Sam's auto repair shop." Bob shrugged. "Monique thinks he's not good enough for Ashley."

Definitely not country club material. But then, neither was Monique. "Why did Ashley start running away?"

Bob's eyes shifted to the side. "The first time was right after Monique and I got married." He sighed. "She accused me of betraying her mother's memory. Resented Monique for trying to take her mother's place. And it doesn't help that Monique has no experience being a parent." He raised his hands, palms up, as if pleading with Bishop to understand. "It's not easy being a stepmother to a teenage girl."

"Yeah, well, I doubt it's easy being a teenage girl, either." Bishop fought the urge to shake his brother. "Why didn't you tell me she was running away?"

"It was a family matter, Tye. Monique doesn't believe in airing our dirty laundry in public."

Bishop stood, tucking his notebook away. He'd thought himself immune to the pain of his brother's betrayal, and yet the words hit him like a sucker punch to the gut. "Wow. A *family* matter, huh?"

Bob jumped to his feet. "I didn't mean it like that."

"Yeah, I'm pretty sure you did. And in case you didn't notice, you just referred to your daughter as dirty laundry." Bishop fought to control his breathing. "Tell me, did Monique even want you to call me?"

Bob looked away. "She thinks Ashley will get over it and come home on her own."

"And you? What do *you* think?"

"It feels different this time," Bob admitted. He continued to glance anywhere other than Bishop. "Ashley and Monique's arguments are usually loud. But this one wasn't. When Monique told her no, Ashley just went to her room. No screaming or slamming doors. First time that's happened."

Bishop waited until Bob's darting gaze finally met his. "Man, what happened to us? We used to be close. And you know I love Ashley like she was my own kid. For the life of me, I can't figure out why you've let Monique drive this wedge between us. Why you allowed her to keep my niece, my *godchild*, from seeing me for the past two years." Bishop stepped toward Bob. "But I'm an adult. I can deal with Monique's guff. But your eighteen-year-old daughter is missing, and you wait four days to ask for my help because your wife didn't want you to? Do you see a problem with that, *Robert*?"

His older brother had always been "Bob" until Monique insisted he be called "Robert." Using that name now, Bishop acknowledged the wedge had done its work. The split between the brothers was complete.

"I'll find Ashley. Not for you. For her, because that kid deserves to know she's the most important person in *someone's* life."

And because he'd been a fool to let anyone stop him from seeing his niece. Maybe if he'd been a better uncle, a true godfather, Ashley would have come to him for help the *first* time she'd run away. And then maybe he wouldn't be here now, feeling like a total failure.

"I need to see her room."

With a defeated nod, Bob led him upstairs, then down a long hall. The closed door at the end bore remnants of Scotch tape and sticky residue.

"What was on her door?" Bishop asked.

"A keep-out sign and some stickers." Bob shrugged. "Normal teen stuff, I guess."

"When did she take it down?"

"She didn't. Monique ripped off the sign, then had our housekeeper remove the stickers as best she could."

"When, Bob?" Bishop repeated the question through gritted teeth.

"Ashley put them up right after we moved here. Monique kept telling her to clean off the door, but Ashley refused. Monique took them down at some point. I don't remember when." Bob turned the knob, pushed the door open and walked into the room.

Bishop followed him in. "Does anything look unusual? Out of place?"

Bob gave the room a once-over, his brows pinched together. "I don't know. I haven't been in here in ages." His gaze landed on Bishop. "I respected her privacy, even after the sign came down."

"She wouldn't let you in even when you knocked and asked permission?" Bishop tried to keep his tone even.

"I gave her some space, Tye." Bob's cheeks reddened. "You've never been a father, so don't judge my relationship with Ashley."

Bishop held his brother's angry glare for a long moment. "Does she still wear that turtle necklace?"

"The one you gave her? She's never taken it off."

Nodding, Bishop said, "You should wait for me downstairs. I need to look around in here by myself."

Bob gave the room another long look, as if it might be his last. Then he left without a word, pulling the door closed behind him.

Bishop stood with his back to the door, taking in a first impression of the entire room. Posters filled two walls. Some were of bands he'd never heard of. There were a few with inspirational quotes, and a couple featured meditation mandalas. He'd taught Ashley a little about mindfulness and meditation. Seeing these posters filled him with the hope that she'd continued to study and find peace through them.

Disregarding his niece's privacy and forcing himself into professional mode, Bishop dug through her dresser drawers, a place where women liked to hide things. After he came up blank, he moved on to her desk. Nothing of interest in the drawers. A docking station sat on top, but the laptop it belonged to was gone. He looked through her closet, not surprised when it yielded no earth-shattering clues.

Bishop's last stop was Ashley's bed. Although the other furniture in the room reflected a young woman on the verge of college, her bed was the one she'd had before her mom died. A twin four-poster, decked out in pink and white ruffles and a canopy stretching above it. Bishop recognized the bed from his visits, back when Bob and Beth had always welcomed him into their home. Ashley was still holding on to her mom through the ruffles and pillow coverings Beth had sewn herself.

He lifted the top mattress and ran his hand between it and the box spring. Ashley hadn't made it easy. She'd hidden the journal there, but on the wall side. He sat on the edge of the bed and opened the hardbound book of teenage trauma.

Skimming past pages of Ashley's heart breaking into pieces on the pages as her mother's health failed, Bishop fought the burning behind his eyes. She'd journaled about forcing herself to keep moving forward because her mother had asked her to. But it had been difficult, according to her entries. She'd tried to find comfort from her father, but apparently Bob was too busy comforting himself.

Several blank pages separated "Before Monique" and "After Monique." Ashley had still been grieving for her mother when Bob interjected Monique into the family. The rest of the entries spoke to Ashley's depression, isolation and longing for love.

Bishop flipped through the pages to the end. There were three last entries, each one addressed to a particular person.

To Dad: I'm sorry, but I just can't live with Monique. You've made it clear that you've chosen her over me. I hope you find happiness together.

To Monique: I wonder what made you so insecure that you feel threatened by my relationship

with my father. Regardless, you win. He's all yours.
Following this entry, a detailed drawing of a hand,
the middle finger pointing up, filled an entire page.

To Uncle Tye: I've only survived this long be-
cause of what you've taught me. I'm sure it's Mo-
nique's doing that I haven't seen you for so long.
You would never abandon me on purpose. Na-
maste.

Bishop's chest ached like he'd just run a mara-
thon. He'd never considered that his niece might
not know why he hadn't visited her all this time. He
wanted to find Ashley all the more, to make sure
she knew that he hadn't abandoned her.

Despite not seeing her for two years, Bishop's
gut told him Ashley might be in real danger. Her
journal entries sounded more like she was running
from her parents than running *toward* anything,
even her boyfriend. And that's when horrible things
could happen to young, vulnerable women. Ashley was looking for love, for comfort. Bishop had
to find her before she found those with the wrong
type of person. The type who preyed on girls like
Ashley.

His fingers curled into fists and he fought the
urge to punch something by shoving them into
his jacket pockets. His right hand brushed up
against the turtle key chain. He held it in a tight

grip, as if it were a talisman that could guarantee his niece's safety.

No matter what it cost him, he would find Ashley and bring her home. He owed her that much.

Chapter Two

Bishop parked in a diagonal space in front of the Boone County Justice Center and climbed out of his pickup. He'd had to exit I-10 west of Houston because of construction, then decided to stay on the longer scenic route the whole way. It added about an hour's drive time, but it was a no-brainer compared to freeway traffic.

Needing to stretch his legs before meeting with the local sheriff, Bishop strolled across the street to the town plaza. Benches sat in the shade of towering live oaks, and the pathways leading to a central fountain were lined with colorful flowers, wilting in the late-summer heat. It wasn't a big park, but then Resolute was a fairly small town for being the county seat.

An elderly gentleman sitting on a bench nodded a friendly greeting and Bishop smiled in return. A far cry from big-city life, where everyone was suspicious of strangers. Or was that just the cynical ex-cop in him talking?

After a brief look around, Bishop headed back

to the justice center. According to his research, the sheriff's office, courthouse and jail were all housed in the three-story structure built around the turn of the century. Well, turn of the *last* century. Hand-hewn native limestone bricks, arched windows with keystones, wraparound balconies on the upper floors. *I bet these walls have some stories to tell.*

While on the Boone County website, he'd also skimmed the sheriff's bio. Wallace Reed had filled the position for the past three decades and then some. There were two possible reasons for that. Either he ran things like a dictator, beating his competitors in election years by nefarious means, or he truly was a good guy and the people around here wanted him right where he was. Giving Sheriff Reed the benefit of the doubt, Bishop climbed the front steps.

Pushing open the heavy wooden door, Bishop was hit by a welcoming blast of air-conditioning. As his eyes adjusted from bright sunlight to the dim interior, he noticed a petite woman with graying hair sitting behind a desk. Her fingers flying across a computer keyboard, she seemed oblivious to his approach. Bishop waited a moment for Helen, according to the nameplate on her desk, to address him.

She didn't.

He cleared his throat. "Morning, Helen. I'd like to speak to Sheriff Reed."

"Have an appointment?" She still didn't bother to glance up from her computer screen.

"I don't." Bishop took in the color-coded file folders standing at attention in an upright holder. A coffee mug bearing the county emblem sat centered on a sandstone coaster. Not a stray paperclip in sight. Bet the old gal ran a tight ship.

A few seconds passed before Helen gave a long-suffering sigh, punched her keyboard one last, forceful time, then deigned to raise her eyes.

Bishop favored her with the full force of his best smile, usually a surefire guarantee of getting one in return.

Helen did not smile back. "The sheriff is extremely busy today."

"It's important. I only need a few minutes." And seriously, how much lawbreaking could be going on in a town this quiet?

She picked up the desk phone's receiver and cocked a brow at him. "Name?"

"Bishop."

"And the nature of your business?" She jabbed one button on the phone.

"I'm looking for someone," he said at the same time Helen spoke into the receiver.

"I'm sorry to bother you, Sheriff, but there's a man here to see you. Says his name is Bishop." Pause. "I *did* tell him you're busy." Helen moved the receiver away from her mouth. "The sheriff wants to know what you're here about."

"It's about a missing person." Bishop answered loud enough for it to carry through the phone.

The sheriff must have heard and issued an order, as the stalwart clerk snapped to. "Right away." With a heavy clank, Helen dropped the receiver in its cradle and stood. "Come with me, please."

Bishop followed her as she marched sharply down a long hallway, her sensible flats making little noise. She stopped at a closed door bearing the words Sheriff Reed, gave one quick rap with her knuckles, opened it and ushered Bishop into the office. As soon as he'd crossed the threshold, Helen pulled the door shut behind her, her soft footsteps fading away.

Bishop's practical joke meter pinged and his smile vanished. *What the...?* The slender redhead standing next to the desk wore a starched white shirt and ironed black jeans. *Who irons creases into their jeans?*

She'd pulled her hair into a high ponytail so tight, he doubted any strand would dare try to slip loose. Almost as tall as Bishop, she was a lot curvier, and her full lips flashed what might have been a quick smile as she sat down and picked up a pen.

"Please have a seat, Mr. Bishop." She motioned to a chair facing her desk. "How can I help you?"

Under other circumstances, Bishop would have several good, if inappropriate, ideas on exactly how she could help him. But with Ashley's whereabouts on the line, he was angry about getting the run-around. "I was under the impression I'd be meeting with Sheriff Reed."

"I *am* Sheriff Reed." Her tone was stern, all business.

"Really?" Bishop crossed the room and dropped into the chair. "Then I can say without a doubt, your picture *really* doesn't do you justice."

Green eyes widened beneath raised brows. "My picture?"

"On the Boone County website? Your profile picture there makes you look a lot older. And definitely more masculine." When she didn't respond, he added, "The website says Wallace Reed is the sheriff. Wild stab here, but I'm guessing you're not Sheriff *Wallace* Reed."

Her eyes closed, and the knuckles gripping the pen whitened until it seemed the poor pen would snap in two. After a deep breath, she opened her eyes, piercing him with a determined stare. "Until a few months ago my father, Wallace Reed, *was* the sheriff. The website hasn't been updated yet, but I assure you, I'm Sheriff *Cassie* Reed. I was appointed after Dad's death."

Bishop gave himself a mental thrashing. An honest mistake on his part, but he regretted joking about what was obviously a deep, personal wound. "I'm sorry for your loss."

Her face devoid of emotion, the sheriff sat taller in her chair. "You said you wanted to talk about a missing person." She flipped her notebook to a fresh page, pen poised to write. "Who *is* the missing person, Mr. Bishop?"

"Just Bishop. No need for the 'mister.'"

She looked up, her glare hardening as she tapped the pen on the paper. Apparently, smiles didn't come easily to the women of Resolute. But even with the glare, *this* woman kicked his resting heart rate up a beat or two.

Bishop tried again. "I'm a private investigator. When I arrive in town, I like to introduce myself. Helps me avoid getting pegged as a peeper or a stalker when I'm on a case. Saves everyone a lot of time and embarrassment."

The sheriff's heart-shaped face tilted ever so slightly to the right. "You're here on a private job?" Bottle-green eyes bored into his with an intensity that held him like a magnet. "Apparently I misunderstood why you wanted to see me. But I certainly appreciate you making me aware of your presence in Resolute. Now, if that's all, Mr. Bishop…"

"Just Bishop. No…" His words tapered off as her eyes narrowed. "Look, I think we got off on the wrong foot. I'm a PI, but this case is personal to me." He leaned forward. "It's my niece who's missing. Her boyfriend's family lives in Resolute, and she may have come here with him. I have their address, but I figured there's a good chance you know them and might be able to give me a little advance intel before I talk to them."

Setting her pen on her desk, the sheriff leaned

back in the chair, her brows drawn together. "I'm sorry to hear about your niece. We take missing persons cases very seriously around here. Especially young girls." Tapping a finger against her generous lips, she seemed lost in thought for a moment. "First, I'd like you to file a report. Then we can discuss approaching the boy's family."

"I already filed the report in Houston, but I doubt much will be done. Ashley's eighteen, and according to her parents, a chronic runaway."

The office door swung open. A young man—dressed like the sheriff right down to the ironed-in creases—leaned into the office. "Hey, sis. You get an ID on our Jane Doe yet?"

"Noah, how many times have I told you about knocking? I'm in a meeting." Her words were reproving but her tone laced with affection.

Noah's eyes flickered to Bishop, then back to his sister. "Sorry. Lonnie needs to know if you still want the sketch artist to work up a drawing of the vic."

"Yes. I haven't heard from the medical examiner yet, but I want the sketch ready in case he can't identify her."

Bishop waited for the deputy to leave. "So, your father *was* sheriff. Now, you *are* sheriff and your brother's a deputy? Let me guess. Lonnie's a brother, too?"

Amusement tugged at one corner of her mouth. Just a hint, but enough to make Bishop hanker to see a full-on smile from her before he left town. "My cousin."

Bishop chuckled. "Does anyone work here who isn't a relative?"

"What can I say? Resolute's a small town, and Boone's a small county." She shrugged. "I apologize for the interruption, but we're in the middle of a murder investigation." She picked up her pen. "Now, please tell me about your niece."

"A murder?" A chill swept through Bishop. "Did that deputy say the vic was female? How old?"

The sheriff stilled, a look of dawning comprehension on her face. "We're not sure." She spoke in a measured tone that Bishop recognized from his days on the force. The tone used to keep victims' families calm. "Teens, maybe early twenties."

Fumbling for his phone, Bishop pulled up a picture and held it out for the sheriff to see. "This is Ashley. She's petite, long blond hair, blue eyes."

Sheriff Reed's full lips tightened into a thin line. When her gaze lifted, Bishop's heart stopped beating and his blood ran cold.

Chapter Three

Waiting for the medical examiner to call back, Bishop almost hyperventilated while doing deep breathing exercises. Even muttering a quiet mantra for Ashley's safety over and over couldn't cut through the overwhelming fear and anxiety clawing apart his insides.

Sheriff Reed grabbed the phone when it rang. "You're positive? I understand. Thank you, Doctor." She ended the call. "The ME confirmed that the vic has no tattoos."

It wasn't Ashley.

Bishop gave a hard bark of laughter. The sheriff probably thought he was crazy, but he didn't care. Now wasn't the time to explain how Monique had screamed like a banshee when Ashley got a small tattoo of a turtle on her ankle a few months earlier. How his brother, so cowed by his own wife that he'd escaped her rantings by meeting Bishop for coffee, had admitted it was actually a cute little tattoo.

Bishop resolved then and there, the first thing on

his agenda after finding Ashley would be getting his own turtle tattoo in celebration of his niece's rebel ways.

To her credit, the sheriff had looked just as relieved as Bishop when the ME said it wasn't Ashley. Bishop had been ready to throw his arms around her, but something about the stiff set of her spine quashed the impulse. Instead, he asked Sheriff Reed about Michael Pugh and his family in Resolute.

"It's just the three boys since the mother died. Mike's in the middle. He's got an older brother, Garrett. Billy's fourteen, maybe fifteen." Her voice, though still matter-of-fact, had softened considerably since Bishop's scare about Ashley and the Jane Doe. Everything about Sheriff Reed screamed tough as nails, but Cassie the woman seemed almost compassionate.

He pulled his notebook from his pocket. "The kids live by themselves?"

"Garrett took custody of Billy when Ms. Pugh died." Cassie shrugged. "The place is paid for, and somehow they find a way to keep the utilities on. Mike used to work at a local garage. Garrett probably does odd jobs or construction work, because I haven't seen him working in town."

Bishop made a note of that. "What about the father?"

"Ms. Pugh never had much luck with men. Each boy has a different daddy, and none of them stuck around much longer than it took to be a sperm donor. Pugh was her maiden name, and she passed it on to her sons."

"The brothers get into trouble much?"

Cassie shook her head. "Some minor drug possession charges on Garrett a few years ago. Nothing on Mike or Billy."

Trying to ignore how the end of her high ponytail swished across her shoulders each time she moved her head, Bishop slapped his notebook closed and stood. "Well, guess it's time to pay them a visit."

"The family's always been downright antisocial." Cassie glanced at her watch, a basic utility model that looked out of place on her slender wrist. "I can't do much on this murder until the autopsy's complete and I get the lab and evidence reports." She stood and came around her desk, a set of keys dangling from her tapered fingers. "I think I'll tag along, if you don't mind. If Ashley *is* in trouble and in my county, I want to know."

"Don't mind in the least." Understatement of the century. Spending the afternoon with the shapely sheriff who got stuff accomplished would be a pleasure. "I'm parked right out front."

"Oh, I'll be driving," Cassie informed him. "No guarantee when it comes to the Pugh brothers, but less chance of my official truck catching a load of buckshot than a stranger's vehicle pulling onto their property."

Grinning, Bishop stepped back and allowed the

sheriff to precede him. He'd enjoy riding shotgun for a change. "Thought you said they weren't troublemakers."

One hand on the door handle, Cassie turned around and caught him staring at her backside.

Bracing for the reprimand he deserved, he thought fast. "I was, uh, just admiring those sharp creases in your jeans."

Although her raised brow told him she didn't buy that for one second, she simply replied, "Having a gun for protection doesn't make someone a troublemaker out here." Cassie's accent thickened like cold honey. "You're not in the big city now, Bishop. Us country folk keep shotguns by the front door." Her eyes sparkled with amusement before she turned and sauntered out of her office.

Her tone was sarcastic, but he didn't care. She'd finally called him Bishop.

"THAT'S THEIR HOUSE up ahead on the left," Cassie told him. They came to a stop along the shoulder of County Road 21, about three miles southwest of Resolute. Three agonizingly slow miles, since the sheriff came to full stops, used her turn signals and obeyed the speed limit even on the empty roads outside of town.

Bishop gazed through the windshield at the small frame house sitting to the side of what looked like a failed town dump. Old tires and a threadbare couch surrounded a rusted-out truck, and smoke wafted up from a burn barrel. "I can see why Michael wanted to try his luck in Houston."

Cassie tapped the gas pedal, easing back onto the blacktop. Pulling into the dirt drive, she stopped behind an old Ford Mustang whose glory days were long gone. When they climbed out of the truck and she slammed her door shut, Bishop shot her a questioning look. In his business, stealth was key.

"Sometimes it's best to let people out here know they have company before you knock on their door." With that bit of advice, she led the way up the porch steps, going around a mangy bloodhound asleep in the shade.

A guy who didn't look much like the pictures Bishop had seen of Michael answered her knock, leaving the screen door closed between them. This Pugh brother had a black eye, swollen lip, and bruises covering his arms and bare chest.

"Hey, Garrett. How y'all doing?" Cassie's tone was friendly, but her back was straight, her shoulders squared.

"Doin' fine, Sheriff. What's up?" His jeans hung low on his hips, the frayed hems bunched under his bare feet.

"Looks like quite a shiner. Hope the other guy looks worse."

Garrett touched beneath his eye and shrugged. "This? This ain't nothin'. Just roughhousing."

Cassie paused, allowing the quiet between them to grow. Bishop knew the tactic. Silence made the person being questioned nervous. But Garrett waited her out, and finally Cassie asked, "Michael home? I need to talk to him."

"What about?" Garrett's gaze slid to Bishop. "Who's this guy?"

"I'm asking the questions, Garrett. Where is Michael?"

"He don't live here no more. Went to Houston after Mama died."

"I heard he came back." Cassie hooked her thumbs on her belt. "Some kind of emergency with you or Billy, as I understand."

Bishop strained to see the dim interior of the room behind Garrett.

Garrett's tongue skimmed over his front teeth, pushing out his upper lip as he looked Cassie over. "No emergency 'round here. We ain't seen Michael for months." He folded his inked arms across his narrow chest, also covered with tats.

Bishop's patience reached its limit. He pulled his phone from his pocket and turned it toward the door. "This is Michael's girlfriend. Did she come by here looking for him?"

The kid squinted at the phone through the dirty screen door, then blinked several times, fast. A tell many liars had. Cassie shifted next to him. The observant sheriff had caught it, too.

"Nope. Never seen her." Garrett swaggered a little, as if emphasizing his claim.

Cassie's smile didn't reach her eyes. "If you see either of them, ask them to give me a call, okay?"

"Sure thing." Garrett pushed the inside door shut before they'd even turned away.

Bishop turned to Cassie, keeping his voice low. "He's lying."

"I know. But we can't force our way inside. There's no indication either one of them is here." Cassie paused before stepping off the porch, raising her voice to a volume that would carry. "Well, if they haven't been here, they haven't been here. Let's go."

Farther up the drive, between the Mustang and a one-car garage, another mutt rolled on his back in the dust. This one looked like a Heinz 57, with short legs, floppy ears and a stub tail. A teenage boy squatted next to him, rubbing the dog's stomach. Bishop headed toward him.

Cassie caught up. "Hey, Billy. Y'all getting along okay without your mom?"

Billy looked up at her. "Yes'm."

"You going to school every day?"

"Don't gotta go. It's out for summer."

She pulled her lips in as if fighting a smile. "I meant during the school year. You keeping up with your classes?"

"Oh. Yeah. I go when I gotta go." Billy's attention returned to the dog.

"I was hoping to catch Michael home."

"Just missed him by a day or so."

Bishop muttered a curse. "He was here?"

Billy's gaze shifted to Bishop, but he spoke to Cassie. "Who's he?"

"A friend." Cassie crouched down to the boy's level. "When was Mike here?"

The kid cocked his head and closed his eyes, his faced scrunched as if it hurt to think. "Got here on the weekend."

Bishop shoved his phone in Billy's face. "Did you see her? Was she here, too?"

After staring at the phone for a full minute, Billy finally nodded. "Yep. She showed up after Mike got here."

Bishop blew out a breath. If Billy were to be believed, Ashley was alive and well. "Do you know where they are now?"

Billy shook his head. "She left. Mike and Garrett had a big fight, then Mike left. Been gone a day or so." Standing, the boy scratched at the acne on his cheek. "Why you lookin' for Mike?"

"He's not in trouble. Just need to ask him something." Cassie straightened. "If you hear from him, tell him to call me, okay?"

Billy shrugged. "Doubt he'll call, but if he does I will."

So Garrett had been lying to them. Bishop couldn't stomach liars at the best of times. Throw Ashley into the mix and he was ready to do some serious damage. He stormed back to the house, taking the porch steps two at a time.

Cassie caught up with him as he pounded his fist against the flimsy door.

When Garrett opened up again, Cassie jumped in before Bishop had a chance to start yelling. "Garrett, I'm about ten seconds away from arresting you for impeding an investigation." Cassie planted her hands on her hips. "I want the truth this time."

"You can't arrest me. I ain't done nothin'—"

"We know Mike and Ashley were here. Where are they?" Bishop gnashed his teeth, fighting the urge to smash his fist square into that belligerent face. "Where'd they go?"

Cassie's threat didn't seem to scare the kid, but Bishop had made grown men cry in interrogation rooms. He'd do the same to Garrett if he didn't start talking. He reached for the screen door handle, but Garrett shoved the whole door at him. The flimsy hinges broke away. Bishop's head popped through the screen and the door frame encircled his shoulders.

Garrett streaked through the house toward the back. As Bishop struggled to get free of the door frame, the edge of it knocked Cassie off balance. Arms pinwheeling, she stepped backward onto the slumbering hound. Baying his indignation, the dog stood and sent Cassie down the steps head over heels.

Bishop, finally free of the door, ran down to help Cassie.

"I'm all right. Go after Garrett." Already on her feet, she charged back up to the porch. "I'll go through, you go around."

Billy stood as Bishop ran past him toward the backyard. The teen signaled him and pointed to the garage. With the small building closed up, Bishop raised his brows in question. Billy motioned for him to go around to the side door.

Cassie skidded to a stop in the backyard. She approached the short chain-link fence that ended at the corner of the garage. Bishop tipped his head toward the garage, and Cassie moved to the side door, behind the fence.

"Are both doors unlocked?" he whispered to Billy.

The kid nodded, and Bishop grabbed the door handle. When Cassie went in from the side, Bishop swung the front door up. Garrett darted out, but Bishop was ready. He caught up with him before Garrett made it past the Mustang, tackling him on the driveway. Bishop flipped him onto his back, holding his scrawny chest down with one hand. He raised the other as if to punch Garrett.

"Dadgummit, Garrett. Why did you run?" Cassie caught up to them.

Bishop held his position but glanced up at Cassie. Did she really just say *dadgummit*?

"I knew this guy was gonna beat me up." Garrett held his hands in front of his face to block any potential blows.

"I'm not going to beat you up unless you keep lying to us." Bishop brandished his fist in the air.

"Okay, okay. They were here. But Mike made me swear not to tell nobody."

"Tell anybody *what*?"

"That they run off together. Said they was gittin' hitched."

"IT MAKES SENSE that Garrett would lie if Mike asked him to." Cassie sipped her sweet tea and looked with disdain at Bishop's unsweetened glass. "The Pugh brothers have always stuck up for each other."

It had taken some convincing, but she'd talked Bishop into grabbing lunch at The Busy B diner. Her stomach had been growling for hours, and she was starting to enjoy the PI's company. Not sure why. She wasn't one to be swayed by a pretty face, but there it was. Bishop's face *was* pretty. And she enjoyed looking at it.

"I don't buy it." Bishop leaned back in the booth, scowling. Even then, he was pretty. "Ashley's not the kind of kid to run off and get married."

Cassie fought the urge to roll her eyes. "But isn't that exactly what she did, and why you're here? She ran off after her boyfriend. Look, she's of age, and at least they're making it legal." Not that getting married was always the best route to take. Her own mother was proof of that.

Marge Dawson, owner of the diner, approached

their table. She not only opened and closed The Busy B every day, but tough times often saw her working the grill and waiting tables during the midafternoon lulls. Though more than twice Cassie's age, Marge served as her sounding board for all matters of a personal nature.

"What'll it be, Cassie darlin'?"

Cassie ordered her favorite, a bacon cheeseburger with fries.

If anything, Bishop's scowl deepened. "You have anything that's not fried or part of a cow?"

Marge's thick caterpillar brows rose sharply as she took in Bishop for the first time. A smile of pure appreciation widened across her face and she patted her tight battleship-gray perm as though primping for a glamour photo. "And who might this be?"

"He's a private investigator from Houston. Just passing through." Cassie kept her tone nonchalant.

"Well, Mr. Fancy Pants." Marge's eyes sparkled with mischief. "We got catfish. It ain't cow, but it *is* fried."

His look of dismay was priceless. "Any chance I could get it grilled? And a dinner salad with balsamic vinaigrette?"

Still smiling, Marge wrote on her pad. "You want a side of bland and tasteless with that?"

Cassie snickered. Loudly. Bishop threw her a scornful look, but she only laughed harder. Imagine Mr. Tough Guy PI being both pretty *and* fussy.

Too bad he'd be leaving town so soon. Might have been fun getting to know him a little better.

She stopped laughing when Bishop morphed from peeved to charming, giving Marge a wicked smile and a playful wink at the same time. "Got to take care of my heart, darlin'. Saving it for my one true love."

Pu-lease. Cassie rolled her eyes so hard, they hurt. But dadgum if Marge didn't fall for that hogwash, hook, line and sinker.

"For you, handsome, anything. I'll toss that sucker on the flattop myself. But I can't promise you'll like it, and no sending it back. I'll bring the *eye-talian* dressing on the side. It may not be up to your standards." The heavyset woman walked away chuckling, her orthopedic shoes squeaking on the bleached linoleum floor.

With no idea what to say after that undisguised display of masculine persuasion, Cassie endured several minutes of awkward silence that settled over the booth.

"If you don't mind, I've got two questions for you." Bishop looked across the table, his expression dead serious.

Cassie blew out a breath of relief at the conversation starter. "Ask away."

"Not sure I ever met a sheriff, or any other officer of the law for that matter, who tripped over a dog, fell down several steps, chased a delinquent and wrapped it all up by saying 'dadgummit.' What's up with that?"

Cassie frowned. "Which part are you confused by? The dog, the steps, the delinquent or the fact that I don't spew profanity?"

"Most cops I know utter a swear word now and then."

"Well, my daddy taught me that ladies don't swear. And that gentlemen don't swear in front of ladies." She aimed a satisfied smile at him. "My brothers learned that by way of a few good swats and several bars of soap. I learned it by way of my brothers getting punished."

"So you never—"

She leaned forward. "Let's get one thing straight right here and now. I'm no shrinking violet who faints at the sight of blood. I can shoot straighter, fight harder and chase down a fugitive faster than anyone in my department, including my brothers and cousin." Her smile had disappeared. "But I don't swear. Now, what's your second question?"

"Why'd they leave the e's off of Bee?"

Cassie threw her head back and laughed. "Okay, first thing you need to know about this place is that Marge is the sole owner, so there's no 'they' making decisions around here. Second, the 'B' doesn't stand for Bee. It stands for Body." Cassie smiled at Bishop's puzzled expression. "Our Marge is ground zero for all gossip and rumors in Resolute and proud of it. So she named the place The Busy Body."

"Makes sense. But if she's so proud of the fact, why not spell out the word?"

"Because the 'y' in Body put it at eleven letters, and the price point she could afford for the sign out front was ten. The Busy Bod sounded wrong in more ways than one, so she just went with B. *And* made the sign guy give her a discount for having only eight letters."

Bishop laughed, his dimples deepening in his five-o'clock shadow.

Like Marge, Cassie felt the full force of those dimples. But no way would she give him the satisfaction of knowing. "You heading back to Houston this afternoon?" She tore into a package of soda crackers to tide her over until the food arrived.

"Why would you think that? I still have to find Ashley."

Pursing her lips, Cassie chose her words with care. "She's eighteen, Bishop. She's got the right to do what she wants, including getting married."

"That's the problem. I'm not sure she's doing what she wants." The words from Ashley's last journal entry haunted him. "There's more to this whole thing."

"I'm just not seeing it. There's no evidence that even hints at your niece being a missing person." She slid over in the booth and turned sideways, stretching her legs out along the seat. "I'd offer to help you keep looking, but I've got my hands full with that murder case." *And trying to break up a human trafficking ring. And figuring out who killed my father.* "Have you considered that you're thinking about this all wrong? Maybe you should be happy for your niece. Maybe Ashley and Mike are simply a modern-day Romeo and Juliet story."

Squeezing lemon wedges into his iced tea, Bishop paused, meeting her eyes. "You do know how that story ended, right?"

Cassie's mouth watered as he crushed the citrus, but it was the flexing tendons in his powerful hand and the scattering of dark hair at his tanned wrist that had her licking her lips. Pretty faces might not turn her head, but she'd always had a thing for masculine hands.

Marge returned with a full tray and set Bishop's food the table. "Catfish, grilled, not fried."

"With a side of bland and tasteless," Bishop added with another wink for Marge.

"And here's your nekked salad, dressing on the side." The Busy B owner cackled with delight. "Get it? It's nekked 'cause it ain't dressed yet."

Bishop laughed with her, revealing yet another facet of his personality. Whether he found her remark funny or not, he made sure Marge thought he did. Cassie straightened in her seat when Marge set the burger and fries in front of her. Dousing everything on her plate with ketchup, she took a huge bite of the burger and held off replying to the

Romeo and Juliet comment until she'd swallowed. With the greasy food filling her stomach, everything seemed right with the world.

"Can I get y'all anything else?"

"I'm good." Bishop forked catfish into his mouth. "This is delicious."

Marge's cheeks blushed red. "Of course it is. I cooked it." With a satisfied nod and grin, she headed to the kitchen.

Cassie turned her attention back to the conversation with Bishop. "Two young lovers eloping doesn't exactly equal tragic death all around. But I understand that you're worried about your niece." The pleading sorrow in Bishop's eyes when he'd thought his niece might be lying in the morgue had pierced her heart.

"That, I am. And by the way, I'm not buying the Romeo and Juliet story. Since Resolute is the last place she was seen, this is where I plan to start digging." Bishop dipped a fork tine into the salad dressing, touched it to his tongue. Pushing the tiny ramekin aside, he dug into the *nekked* salad. "I appreciate your help today, and I get it that you're busy. I actually prefer working cases on my own." Around a mouthful of greens, he added, "I do have a favor to ask, though."

Eyeing his healthy lunch with distaste, Cassie dragged a fry through the puddle of ketchup and popped it into her mouth. "I'm listening."

"Run a trace on Ashley's cell phone for me."

Cassie stopped midway from popping another fry into her mouth. *Seriously?* She dropped the fry on her plate. Wiping greasy fingers on a paper napkin, Cassie shook her head. "You know I can't do that, Mr. Bishop. Just as I presume you know that you can't officially make the request since you don't own the phone."

"You can run it if she's in imminent danger." He seemed oblivious to her now-frosty demeanor.

"There *is* no imminent danger that I'm aware of. Garrett told us she eloped. I have no reason to doubt that." This is why pretty faces rarely did anything for her. They almost always spelled trouble.

Despite her irritation, the hunch of his shoulders and slight rounding of his eyes tugged at her heart. Still…

"Garrett's a liar. Billy's fourteen and just repeating what Garrett told him. How's that for doubt?"

"I'll grant you that. But based on what I know, it would be against the law for me to trace her phone, and you know it." She pushed her plate to the side, her appetite gone. He probably wouldn't believe her, but she was well acquainted with the frustration of being thwarted at every turn while trying to find a loved one. But the law was the law.

"Then at least issue be-on-the-lookout orders for Michael and Ashley's vehicles. If they ran off together, it makes no sense that both cars are gone."

"If they don't plan to come back to Resolute, it makes perfect sense that they took both vehicles."

Cassie flagged down Marge for the check. "Most likely they'll head back to Houston. They might already be there by now." She eyed Bishop, whose mesmerizing dimples had been vanquished by disappointment. "Have you checked with her father?"

"My brother would have called me if she'd shown up. *Especially* if she'd shown up married." Bishop ran his fingers through his thick hair, leaving it standing out at odd angles that somehow charmed her and threatened to undo her resolve. "Why can't you just do me a solid and put out the BOLOs?"

"Because I have no legal cause to do that." Cassie bristled. He was pushing too hard. Time to push back. "Listen up, because I won't say this again. I don't break the law. Not for anyone."

Bishop's laugh lacked any trace of humor. "Seriously? You're telling me that you've never given a shoplifter a second chance? Coached someone giving a statement to make sure their attacker went to jail?"

Heat flooded Cassie's face. "I absolutely have not. What kind of sheriff do you think I am?" She stood, furious with him for even suggesting such things. But as she threw a twenty on the table, her anger turned toward herself. She should have known as soon as her stomach started fluttering like a dadgum hummingbird that he'd be no good for her. "And if you'd ever been a real cop, instead of just some private *dick*, you'd understand how important it is to follow the law. To the letter, *Mister* Bishop."

With that pronouncement, she strode toward the door, leaving him in the booth with no regrets.

Chapter Four

Well, *that* didn't end well.

Bishop took another sip of iced tea and leaned back in the booth. Not that he cared what Cassie Reed thought about his career choice. She was wrong, though, about him not knowing how crucial cops' rules were. He knew firsthand.

Crucial in screwing up investigations.

Crucial in getting a confidential informant killed.

Crucial in pushing a reputable detective to the brink of rage and madness.

He had only agreed to pause for lunch with the hope that he could enlist the sheriff's help. He'd been an idiot to think that a small-town sheriff might not be such a stickler for all those stifling rules. That maybe, just maybe, she'd be willing to extend him a little professional courtesy and bend the rules to make sure Ashley was found safe. It wasn't as if he'd asked her to do more than cut through the red tape.

At least now it was clear that he'd be on his own,

and that was just fine with him. That clear-eyed, fresh-faced beauty with all those womanly curves was just another by-the-booker. He knew the type and wanted no part of it. Besides, working with her would only distract him as her scent, that of a warm summer evening washed clean by rain, enveloped him. Bishop dug his wallet out of his back pocket and added another twenty to the one Cassie had left.

Marge's rubber-soled squeak announced her arrival. "Hold on, Fancy Pants." She picked up the cash. "I'll get you your change. Just be a minute."

"Keep it. I appreciate the special order."

Marge's eyes widened, as did her smile. "That's mighty kind of you, sir." She waved the money in her fist. "Tip like this, and I'll happily serve up bland and tasteless anytime you want. If you're not planning on leaving town, that is." Giving him a taste of his own medicine, she favored him with a conspiratorial wink.

Marge might shuffle along like an old lady in her orthopedic shoes, but there was nothing wrong with her hearing.

"As a matter of fact, I was wondering if you could recommend a good motel in town. Maybe something with a small fridge in the room?"

"I can do you one better." Marge flopped down opposite Bishop in the booth, letting out a loud sigh. "Lordy, it sure does feel good to get off my feet for a minute. Must have been crazy, opening a diner in this economy. Can't even afford to hire full-time help." She grabbed a napkin from the dispenser and wiped down the salt and pepper shakers before setting them back in their wire holder. "Now, the place you want to stay is Doc's Motor Court, out on the west edge of town. Just take Main Street to Pecan and hang a right. Can't miss it. He's got a row of rooms, but trust me, you don't want none of those."

"I don't?" Bishop relaxed against the booth back. The engaging conversation with Marge washed away the bitter taste left in his mouth after his encounter with the sheriff.

"'Course not. You'll be wanting one of them detached kitchenettes. That's where you'll get your refrigerator and coffee maker. Even a microwave and electric burner." She folded her arms across her full bosom. "Be gettin' a lot more privacy that way, too. The walls in them row rooms are as thin as cardboard. Guy in the next room farts, you'll be waving your hand in front of your nose."

Bishop chuckled at Marge's colorful way of expressing herself. Not like the uptight sheriff. "Gotcha."

"I'm dead serious. If Doc tries to stick you in one of them, you tell him I said to put you in his best detached or he's cut off for a month."

"Cut off?" Bishop's smile wavered. "From eating here?"

Marge tipped her head back, roaring with laughter until she sputtered and gasped for breath.

Bishop leaned across the table. "You all right? Do you need anything? Water? A pat on the back?"

His questions set her off again. "Whooee! I ain't had a laugh that good since I don't know when." Marge pulled a paper napkin from the holder and wiped tears from her eyes. "Me and Doc are married, ya see. And just 'cause we ain't exactly spring chickens don't mean we stopped having fun in the sack. *That's* what I meant by cut off." Her chortles tapered off.

Bishop adored Marge's candidness. "I figured that's what you meant. I just didn't want to assume—"

"Hogwash. You young'uns think passion dies at fifty. You'll learn differently someday." Marge gave Bishop a sharp nod. "Now then, back to the motor court. Doc's may not have a swimmin' pool or one of them free breakfast spreads, but it's cheap, clean, and has everything you'll need. Just promise me you'll come by here once in a while for some good, old-fashioned home cookin'. Don't just be nuking junk food in the microwave."

"Appreciate the recommendation, Marge. And I promise to eat—" Bishop tapped the Formica tabletop twice "—right here as often as possible. If the sheriff doesn't run me out of town first."

Marge reached over and patted his hand. "Don't

you judge our Cassie too hard. There are reasons she's the way she is."

"I don't mean to judge her at all. But you have to admit, she is a bit…rigid."

"Rigid?" Marge snickered. "Oh, come on. Call it what it is. That girl's got a stick so far up her butt, it must tickle her tonsils. She just needs to loosen up and have some fun." She cocked her head to the side, scrutinizing Bishop's face. "And you might be just the fella to make that happen."

Bishop snorted.

Shaking her head, Marge pushed herself up from the booth, groaning with the effort. "Don't laugh it off just yet. You'll see. I'm right about darn near everything."

So thought almost every woman Bishop had ever known. But Marge didn't deserve the sharp edge of his cynicism, so he kept the snide remark to himself. Instead, he thanked her and left the diner.

A wave of heat blasted him as he eyed the parking spaces, remembering he'd left his truck at the justice building. With a groan, he began the sweltering trek back to his truck. Burning him up more than any blazing sun was the sheriff's refusal to trace Ashley's phone or put out the BOLOs. Two small asks that would've given him a jump start in his search and saved him crucial time.

Rounding a corner, Bishop paused in the shade of a shop's awning and pulled his phone out to check it. A couple missed calls from unknown numbers, but no voice messages. He scanned the list of new emails, none of them urgent. Several texts from Bob, sending the most recent pictures of Ashley he could find, as Bishop had requested. He clicked on one of the photos to enlarge it. He stared at the dark blue eyes that ran in his family, the innocent smile of a happy teenager. Or had Ashley just pretended to be happy for the picture, hiding her true emotions behind the smile? Hiding them within the pages of her journal?

Bishop's chest tightened, and he continued toward his truck, his long strides eating up the distance. He'd wasted precious time stopping to eat with the sheriff, and all for nothing.

He'd find Ashley, and he didn't need Cassie Reed to do it.

A TWINGE OF guilt hit Cassie as she parked next to Bishop's truck in front of the justice center. The late August heat rose from the street in shimmering waves. He'd be lucky not to blister his feet right through his boot leather walking here from the diner.

But she didn't feel guilty enough to go back for him. She should have known he'd be like all the other men she'd been attracted to. Only interested in the easy way, not the right way.

Pushing through the front door, a blast of air-conditioning raised goose bumps on her arms.

"Whew! Feels good in here." She approached Helen's desk. "What do I need to know?"

"Sean, Dave and Noah are canvassing the neighborhood around the stash house again." Helen glanced at her desk calendar, where she faithfully kept track of all comings and goings of the deputies. "Lonnie's following up a lead on the victim, Adam's out on a vandalism call, and Pete's hanging around the bullpen in case any calls come in."

Already moving toward her office, Cassie U-turned as Helen's words sank in. "Lonnie has a lead on the victim?"

"He provided no other information, just that he'd be gone for a while."

"Hmm." Curiosity crawled through Cassie. Could Lonnie be close to discovering who their Jane Doe was? All they knew so far was that she wasn't local. None of her deputies had recognized the young woman from the crime scene photos, and no one from Resolute had been reported missing. If they were lucky, the victim's identity would lead them straight to the traffickers. Shutting down those degenerates was consuming her, much as it had her father. *What had Dad discovered that led to him being gunned down?*

"Notify the deputies, please." Cassie checked her watch. "Full team meeting at three o'clock sharp. We need to update one another and strategize a new game plan for these traffickers." She smoothed back the already taut hair at her temples, then winced when Helen's stiff brows arched at the telling gesture.

"What's got you more agitated than usual?" the older woman asked, never pausing as she straightened a stack of reports and placed them in her filing basket. The one attempt to hire a file clerk had ended with the clerk quitting in tears after Helen criticized the girl's work ethic and inability to grasp a basic understanding of the alphabet. Even Cassie steered clear of the file room out of fear of messing up her system.

Cassie jerked her hand away from her hair. "We clearly have a leak, and I can't be sure that it isn't the reason our Jane Doe is dead."

"There's no evidence to support that thinking, so stop adding stress to a plate already full of real issues." Helen slid a file drawer closed with a *thunk*. "What did you learn at the Pugh house?"

"At first, Garrett claimed he hadn't seen Mike *or* the girl. We talked to Billy outside, and he told us Mike and Ashley *had* been there. Apparently, it caused quite a row between Mike and Garrett. You should have seen Garrett's face. What a mess."

"Odd that he lied about seeing them." Helen rose to sort through a stack of files on the credenza behind her desk.

"That's what we thought, too. When we went back to the house to talk to Garrett again, he took off like the bogeyman was on his heels. And that's after he clobbered Bishop with the screen door."

"He's just 'Bishop' now?" Helen kept her tone neutral, but arched her brow again. Sometimes it was doggone annoying working with people who knew you so well. "And he got clobbered with a screen door?" She shrugged as she handed Cassie several case files. "Never a dull moment with those Pugh boys. Did you find out why Garrett lied?"

"He told us Mike and Ashley ran off to get married. Allegedly, Mike made him promise not to tell anyone." Cassie turned away, then turned back. "I'll be in my office. If *Mr.* Bishop happens to show up, ask him to leave a message. I have work to do." She held up the case files.

She'd taken only three steps toward her office when Helen said, "So it's like that, is it?"

Cassie whipped around. "Like *what*, Helen?" The unsuccessful raid and a dead Jane Doe. A possible leak. Garrett's hinky behavior. Bishop's casual request that she break the law. And now this. She was not in the mood.

Helen stood taller and raised her chin. "You've no cause to take that tone with me, Cassie Reed. You may be my boss, but I've been looking out for you since the day your mother took off. Tell me to mind my own business if you want, but the least you can do is use a civil tone while you're doing it."

Cassie drew in a deep breath, then exhaled slowly. "You're right. I apologize. And it is none of your business."

"I figured that would be your attitude."

Lord, give me patience. "Okay, out with it. I'll get no peace until you do."

Helen settled her skinny butt in her chair. "Electricity was crackling between you two before you even walked out the door this morning. Now you're avoiding him, hiding out in your office."

"As you said yourself, I've got a lot on my plate right now. The last thing I need is to get involved—"

"Think about it, Cassie." Helen held up one finger. "Eyes bluer than a Texas swimming hole." She added another finger. "Dimples for days." Third finger. "And he'll be leaving town sooner or later. Sounds like the perfect man for you."

"What's that last one supposed to mean?" Cassie crossed her arms. "Leaving town sooner or later?"

Helen scoffed. "I've known you since you were knee-high to a grasshopper. You've never been in a relationship that wasn't over before it started." She shrugged her bony shoulders. "You're the love-'em-and-leave-'em queen of Boone County."

Even the icy air-conditioning couldn't mitigate the heat flowing through Cassie. "That's not true. And I don't appreciate—"

Helen held her hands up in a defensive position. "I couldn't have worked for your father for so many years without coming to know and care about you and your brothers. So anything I say is said out of love." Her eyes softened, draining the ire out of Cassie.

"I know." Cassie bit her lip. Helen had always been the one she'd turned to when she needed advice from a woman. Advice on raising three younger brothers. Advice on the facts of life when she'd hit puberty. "But I *don't* love 'em and leave 'em."

"No, technically *they* leave because you always choose men who are just passing through."

"Well, it would be pretty darn awkward living in a small town full of exes."

There went Helen's judgy brow again.

"I just haven't found the right man yet."

"Whatever you say, sweetie." With a knowing smile, Helen lowered her gaze back to her computer screen.

Cassie huffed and strode toward her office.

"You keep rolling your eyes like that, they're gonna get stuck." Helen's singsong voice followed her down the hall.

Closing her office door, Cassie tossed the files on her desk and crossed the room. The justice center's architecture reflected an era when buildings were designed with character, rather than today's sleek lines of steel and glass. As a result, she was blessed not with a sterile, fluorescent-lit workplace where so many in law enforcement spent their days, but a spacious corner office with magnificent windows on two walls.

Desperate for a moment to gather her thoughts, she stared across at the empty town square. After

8:00 p.m., when evening came and the temperature finally dropped below ninety degrees, the grassy, tree-lined square would fill with people walking dogs, pushing strollers or just enjoying the fresh air. Cassie often joined in, finding contentment mixing with the townsfolk. Her dad had taught her that good peace officers didn't just protect their town, they participated in it.

A flash of movement caught her eye, and just like that, her growing sense of calm evaporated. Bishop hustling toward his truck. Jaywalking. She might have known. Helen may know nothing when it came to Cassie's relationships, but she was on the mark when it came to the intriguing PI. He was definitely easy on the eyes. And he could probably charm the dew off the honeysuckle.

Well, she wasn't honeysuckle. And she dang sure wasn't Marge, cooking special meals after getting suckered by a pretty face. Even Helen seemed to soften where Bishop was concerned. Well, not her. Not with his lack of ethics. The man didn't seem to know how wrong things could go when the rules weren't followed. But Cassie did. All too well.

As Bishop approached, he looked directly at her window. The sun reflecting off the glass must surely prevent him from seeing her. Then again, maybe not. For at that very moment he raised his arm and waved at her, flashing that dimpled grin.

Startled, Cassie jerked away from the window, then immediately berated herself. It wasn't

as though she'd been watching for him. She'd
chewed him out at the diner, so what in tarnation were the wave and grin about? Probably a
sorry attempt to get under her skin even more.
Not likely, Mr. *Bishop.*

She stepped back to the window, catching a
glimpse of his truck backing up, then peeling out
with a screech of rubber on hot pavement. She
didn't know where he was going in such an all-
fire hurry, but Resolute had speed limits. Shaking
her head with annoyance, Cassie stepped over to
her desk and dropped into the well-worn leather
executive chair. It had been her dad's, as had the
desk, and the office, for longer than she'd been
alive. When the county council had chosen her to
take over as sheriff a few months earlier, she'd considered getting a new chair. Or at least moving the
one she'd used as chief deputy into this office. But
she couldn't bring herself to do it.

The first time Cassie had sat on the leather seat
and run her hands over the scuffed wooden arms,
the legacy of Wallace Reed had flowed into her.
She'd learned from the best sheriff this county had
ever known, and she'd resolved to keep his office
exactly as he'd left it. His ethereal presence lingered, guiding her, giving her the confidence to
solve his murder and shut down the traffickers.

Cassie spent the next hour reviewing crime
scene reports from the raid. The forensic investigators in Austin were processing all the evi-

dence since Boone County had no specialists of its own. There'd been so many items collected, not everything had been tested yet. Despite numerous fingerprints at the location, so far there were no matches in the databases. DNA results from still-viable body fluids wouldn't be back anytime soon. Other items collected—a few loose coins, one black hoop earring etched with skulls, and a pocketknife—were waiting for the overworked techs to examine.

Exhaling in frustration, Cassie unlocked her top-left desk drawer and pulled out the file on her father's murder. He'd been shot to death in what was clearly an ambush, set up on a call about the trafficking case. She reread the report every few days, each time hoping to find some small detail that she might have overlooked.

Helen's buzz interrupted her futile search.

Cassie punched the intercom button. "Yes?"

"Everyone's back. They're waiting for you in the briefing room."

"Be right there." Cassie closed her father's file, placed it back in the drawer and locked it. She rose and headed to the small conference room they used for briefings, the muscles across her shoulders achingly tight. Plug the leak and shut down the traffickers, and she might finally learn who had brutally shot her father. Nothing else mattered.

Chapter Five

Cassie entered the room flushed with renewed purpose. Lonnie stood at the end of the first table, his right foot on a chair as he leaned forward, speaking with Pete. Noah sat on the other side of Pete, chin to chest, arms crossed, and legs stretched out and crossed at the ankles. He appeared to be dozing. *Gonna have to have a talk with that boy.* At the second table, Sean and Adam sat with an empty chair between them. Each had an open folder before them, studying the papers spread out on the table. Dave, as expected, sat alone at the far end of that table.

Cassie stepped to the lectern and set her own folder down. The room was small enough that she didn't need a microphone, and when she cleared her throat all chatter ceased.

"Noah?" Her loud voice startled him awake. "Will you please take notes on the whiteboard?"

"Huh? Sorry." He rubbed the sleep from his eyes and made his way to the large board at the front. "Guess the heat got to me some."

Dave snickered. "Heat didn't bother Sean or me none."

"That's because you—" Noah started.

"That's enough!" Cassie's voice reverberated around the room. Then at normal volume, she said, "I want to go over yesterday's raid and review everything we have on the victim and scene." She glanced at Dave Sanders, their newest deputy, and the last one her dad had hired. It wasn't his slight frame, thick glasses and pale skin that made Cassie question his career choice. It was his seemingly total lack of common sense. "I know you stayed here to answer calls during the raid, Dave. But I assume you've familiarized yourself with the case details by now."

Dave, slouched in his chair, nodded.

Normally easygoing with her deputies, today Cassie's tone was stern. "I've reviewed the evidence reports. So far, not much to go on, but the investigators still have a lot to wade through." Her gaze swiveled to Adam. "Any updates from the ME's office? Have they ID'd the girl?"

Adam straightened in his chair. "Not yet. I checked again just before the meeting, and they said they'd contact us as soon as they learn anything."

Pursing her lips, Cassie nodded. Some things were beyond their control. Her gaze lit on Lonnie. If his lead on the vic had turned up anything he would've told her immediately, so she continued with the other deputies' reports and left Lonnie's for last. "Sean. Y'all learn anything new during the neighborhood canvass?"

The no-nonsense deputy stood as if still in the military. It was the one habit he couldn't seem to break, and it sure wasn't one to complain about. "Yes, ma'am." He pulled out his pocket notebook and flipped it open. "Approximately one week ago, the neighbor across the alley behind the stash house, a Mrs. Crenshaw, saw a box truck in the alley, backing in and across the yard until it was right up tight to the house. She heard the backup warning and wondered why it was beeping for so long. Said the truck had to maneuver for a while to avoid taking down any fences."

Cassie motioned Noah to write this information on the whiteboard. "I don't suppose she caught a plate number or a description of the driver?"

"No, ma'am. But she said the back bumper was dented in on the driver side, and there was a logo on the side of the truck." Sean referred back to his notes. "Victoria Appliance Sales." He sat, his back still ramrod straight.

"Nothing out of the ordinary about that. Most folks in Resolute order stuff like appliances and furniture from Victoria." Dave added his two cents. "It's a lot closer than San Antonio."

Noah's mouth dropped open as he turned toward his fellow deputy. "Way to miss the point, Dave. There weren't any new appliances in that house."

"Or empty spaces left by repossessed ones." Sean shook his head at the newbie. "Think before you open that big yap of yours, Sanders."

"I was just stating a fact, *Cavanaugh*. Remember, I had to stay here while you guys went on the raid. How am I supposed to know what was or wasn't in the stupid house?" Dave crossed his arms.

"Dave, it seems you just stated a fact that proves you did *not* read the reports." Cassie gripped the edge of the lectern. She needed to pair the newbie up with an experienced partner and hope he increased his street smarts. "But we'll discuss that later. Privately."

He aimed a sullen glare at his boss.

"Let's get back on track, shall we?" Cassie turned again to Sean. "How long was the truck parked at the back door? And no need to stand this time."

Sean answered without glancing at his notes. "It came in late evening and was gone by the next morning. She didn't see it leave."

"That explains why we didn't see it when we staked out the house." Peter so seldom spoke during briefings that everyone paid attention when he did. "We made note of all passenger vehicles coming and going before the raid. They all checked out. Besides, we knew it was too risky to move the girls individually, so we figured they were in something bigger. We never caught a van or box truck anywhere near the house."

Only once had Cassie been on a stakeout with Pete. One of the most boring nights of her life. The man was an enigma, keeping his own counsel even more than she did.

Noah moved away from the whiteboard and grabbed his notebook. "I can confirm that account of a late-night delivery truck. Um, give me a sec." Flipping pages for a few moments, Noah finally found what he sought. "Here it is. Mr. Boyd Jackson, who lives next door to the stash house, said it was full-on dark. He couldn't make out the logo, and when the driver opened the double back doors, they almost touched the house. He couldn't see what they were loading or unloading, but he knew the house was empty. Thought maybe the owner hired a cleaning crew or renovation company. He did think it was odd, it happening so late at night."

Cassie cocked a brow at Noah and waved a hand toward the board. "This is good work, Noah. Write it down." Hoping for more useful tidbits, she asked, "Did we find anyone who *heard* anything?"

Noah finished writing before turning back toward the others. "Yeah, Mr. Jackson's wife. She said that same night, after they'd gone to bed, she awoke to the sound of cats."

"Cats?" Dave's sarcastic tone made Cassie close her eyes for a moment. Although Noah had been on the force longer and had more experience, Dave was older. For some reason he seemed to think he was entitled to better assignments than Noah and took out his frustration verbally. She needed to shut that down, and quick.

"Yeah, *cats*." Noah glared at Dave. "She said she got up in the middle of the night and thought she heard a child crying. But it was off and on, sometimes more than one at a time. She finally decided it had to be feral cats in the alley."

Noah wrote "Cats!" on the board with no urging from Cassie.

"Helen said you were chasing a lead on the victim?" Cassie asked Lonnie.

"I thought she might be a dancer at Bush Whackers out on State Highway 87. Drove out there, talked to Shorty, but he said he hadn't hired anyone new."

Adam leaned forward to smirk down the row at Lonnie. "Fess up, Dixon. You were just getting your jollies while the rest of us were working."

Everyone, including Lonnie, laughed. "Hey, I take my job very seriously."

Cassie allowed the moment before moving on to the next subject. "Okay, time to address the elephant in the room." Frustration was burning a hole in her stomach. "Yesterday's raid was my first since becoming sheriff, and it went south. Three more like it when my father ran things. This many is no coincidence, which means we have a leak."

This brought her team to their feet, voicing loud, indignant denials. Cassie raised her hands. "All right, all right. Settle down. You can't tell me I'm the only one to draw this conclusion." Her men reluctantly took their seats and the room finally quieted.

Lonnie broke the silence, his voice cold. "Are you saying someone in this room is dirty?"

"No, I'm not. I trust every man in this room with my life. The leak could be coming from other sources." She paused. Though she believed what she'd just said in her heart, she knew she couldn't rule out a leak among her group. She just wasn't about to announce that worry. "Anyone have any thoughts?"

"My money's on Judge Harmon's office," Sean said. "He issues the warrants, and that man's known for his indiscretions, especially when he's had too much to drink."

"Which is pretty often," Pete added.

Adam shrugged. "Could be someone in clerical, maybe."

"Possibly," Cassie agreed. "I'll speak to Helen. She knows everyone in the building."

"Have you asked Marge if she's heard any rumors?" Noah asked. "If anyone knows something, it would be her."

"I don't discuss ongoing cases with anyone. And especially now, none of you better, either." Cassie went eye to eye with each man to emphasize her words. "Besides, Marge would have told me if she'd heard about anything hinky going on."

Cassie's cell phone vibrated. She pulled it from her pocket and read the text from Helen.

Two Texas Rangers waiting for you. They don't look happy.

"Meeting adjourned."

CASSIE SETTLED INTO her office chair before calling Helen.

"Please bring them back."

"Yes, ma'am." The line went dead.

A moment later a sharp rap on the door sounded and Helen entered ahead of two tall, lean men wearing the prerequisite Stetsons and silver cinco-peso badges. "Ranger Ward." She tipped her head toward the man to her right.

"Ma'am." He removed his hat to reveal cropped sandy blond hair.

Before Helen could introduce the man to her left, he stepped forward, also removing his hat. "Ranger Mills, Sheriff."

"Thank you, Helen. Gentlemen, have a seat and tell me what I can do for you."

Both men sat, resting their Stetsons on their laps. They waited until Helen left the room, pulling the door closed behind her.

Ward took lead. "Sheriff Reed, are you aware of a human trafficking ring operating within Boone County?"

"I'm well aware. We've been tracking their movements for some time," she acknowledged. "In fact, just yesterday—"

"Let me stop you there, Sheriff," Ward interrupted, the frown lines between his brows deepening. "We're not here to work on the trafficking case."

"Not directly," Mills added.

Cassie cocked a brow and waited.

Ward resumed. "We've received information that someone is tipping off the traffickers. Letting them know when raids will take place, among other things."

Shocked that the Rangers knew about the leak, Cassie's pulse quickened. "Yes, my father, the former sheriff, came to the same conclusion. We were working that angle when he was killed." Cassie cleared her throat of the telling emotion. It was still hard to talk about her father's death. "Are you here because you know who the leak is? Or do you need my help finding the source? Because, gentlemen, if we plug this leak, then shutting down those traffickers just got a whole lot easier."

Neither Ranger had smiled since entering her office. Maybe they never smiled. But now, their mouths pinched into tight, straight lines, they both looked downright grim.

There's more going on here than they're telling me. Cassie held their gaze as good as she got. "We going to sit here all day, or are you going to tell me why you're really here?"

Mills looked to Ward, who nodded ever so slightly. "We have information that suggests the leak is someone within these walls."

Cassie leaned against the back of her chair, hands in her lap. "We've considered that and are currently investigating it. It's quite possible someone within the clerical office or judge's chambers—"

"We're not talking about the entire building," Mills said.

Cassie's fingers curled into fists, the short nails digging into her palms as a visceral dread ran through her. It unsettled her to think a member of her team could be responsible for tipping off the bad guys. She sure as heck didn't want to share that worry with outsiders. If it was someone she trusted, she needed to track them down on her own and deal with it. By the book, yes, but with fairness. Her team was family in more ways than one.

"As of this moment," Ward added, "you and your deputies are no longer authorized to work on the trafficking case. All related files will be confiscated and online access denied until we've completed a full investigation of the Boone County Sheriff's Department." He handed her an envelope he'd been holding beneath his hat. "This gives us the authority."

She snatched the offending paper from his outstretched hand, fighting the urge to rip it to shreds.

"This is ridiculous. It's obvious that your informant is playing you for fools."

"Ma'am, we take corruption very seriously and would advise you to do the same." Ward stood. "We require space in the building to work from." He opened her office door and paused, as if expecting her to jump up and fulfill his demand.

Cassie made no move to stand. "If you'll both have a seat in the reception area, I'll see what I can find." She caught the look that passed between the two men, and Ward's scowl filled her with a petty satisfaction.

"We'd like to get started as soon as possible." He exited her office, Mills on his heels.

Cassie could barely breathe. Her palms throbbed where her nails had drawn blood. Ward said they weren't going after the trafficking ring themselves. Pulling her whole department from the case would give the traffickers free rein to cross through her county.

She needed to find the real culprit responsible for the leaks.

But first things first. Cassie punched the phone button for Helen and asked her to come to her office. Between the two of them, they'd find the perfect space for the Rangers to use. She was pretty sure a corner in the basement was available.

Chapter Six

Bishop chuckled to himself as he climbed into his truck. He'd barely glimpsed Cassie's face at the window, but the flash of red hair had given her away. He wouldn't mind getting to know the vexing sheriff a little better, but finding Ashley was his number one priority. Too bad Cassie wasn't willing to cut a bureaucratic corner or two to assist.

Bishop drove southwest out of town, intent on questioning Garrett again, this time without the inflexible sheriff looking over his shoulder. But when he approached the house, a faded red Corolla was parked in the driveway behind the old Mustang. Unable to stake out the house without being made, he braked, took a picture of the car's plate and headed back to Resolute. Best to identify Garrett Pugh's visitor before getting in the kid's face again.

After making a few stops in town for necessities, Bishop followed Marge's simple directions to the motel. Doc's Motor Court looked to be straight out of a movie from the fifties. The facade above the office arched over the driveway to connect with a thick stucco wall surrounding the property. Just as engaging as his wife, Doc talked his ear off while checking Bishop into one of the stand-alone kitchenettes.

He hauled his bags inside the sweltering room as quickly as possible and cranked the window unit to high. After stripping down to boxers and socks, he crammed his groceries into the small fridge and set his new smoothie blender on the counter. Still sweating, he dropped into the chair by a small table.

It had been a long day, and he wasn't any closer to finding Ashley. He rubbed his chest just above the sternum, trying to ease a tightening band of anxiety. Anxiety he hadn't experienced since leaving the police force.

Pulling his laptop from the duffel bag, he powered it on and plugged in the Toyota's license plate. Technically, he shouldn't run searches on vehicles not directly related to a case he was working. But Bishop didn't pay attention to many technicalities.

Armed with the owner's name, he started a background check. Turned out Kevin Palmer was quite an enigma. Born in El Paso, his past addresses included San Antonio, Midland and Fort Stockton. He was currently renting a house in Flowertop, a small town not far from Resolute. His spotty work history consisted of short-term stints in manual labor.

Although the employment gaps could have valid explanations, they nagged at Bishop once he linked them to corresponding stretches when Palmer's Texas driver's license was expired. The man might have just moved out of state during those periods, but Bishop's gut said Palmer had been doing time.

Bishop pulled up the Texas DPS Crime Records database and tried to log in. After exceeding his password attempts, he remembered he'd changed it recently. Calling to reset it meant working his way through an automated list of options longer than a country block. It would be faster to request the records in person.

He pulled on his T-shirt and jeans and jogged to his truck. If he calculated correctly, he should make it to the justice center right before it closed, though he may have to break the local speed limit to do it. That didn't matter. If Palmer had a criminal record, Bishop would have a copy of it by end of day.

"THIS ROOM SHOULD be fine for them." Helen had vetoed the basement, suggesting instead a large unused office in the back of the building. "I'll have a second desk moved in. There's plenty of space."

Cassie eyed the old desk and rickety chair already in the room. "Fine. And since you insist on keeping them up here, maybe you could swing by a few times throughout the day, ask if they'd like coffee or something."

Helen's eyes widened. "Well, let's just take a giant step backward in women's equality, shall we?"

"I'm not asking you to wait on them." Cassie chuckled at the indignant expression on Helen's face. "But if you have an excuse to loiter outside their door from time to time, you might pick up some intel."

"I'll be sure to keep my ear to the ground." She patted Cassie's arm as they walked toward the front lobby. "Don't worry. I'm sure they're wrong about our department. If not, they'll find the leak *for* you. Either way, they'll be gone before you know it."

Less than an hour later, Helen was eating her words.

BISHOP THANKED THE clerk for the printed copy of Palmer's report. She gave him a tight smile that lasted only long enough to close up her station, muttering something under her breath about people waiting until closing time.

Bishop's own smile faded as he lowered himself onto a bench in the lobby, reading Kevin Palmer's rap sheet.

The man had spent more than half of his thirty-eight years behind bars. His most recent stint ended about a year ago. The arrests corresponded to Palmer's addresses on record. El Paso, San Antonio and again in El Paso. The crimes included felony shoplifting, possession with intent to distribute, assault, assault with a deadly weapon, and sexual assault.

Palmer had roofied a young woman, then raped her after she was passed out. She'd been nineteen. He'd been thirty-one. Five years in prison for ruining a life before it had barely started. Palmer had claimed the sex was consensual and his buddies backed up his testimony. After the victim had filed the police report and put herself through the added trauma of an exam and evidence collection, she'd refused to testify. Palmer's friends had most likely scared the ever-loving daylights out of her, threatening her life as well as her family's if she showed up in court. He'd seen it more times than he liked to count during his days on the force.

But even without the victim's testimony, the rape kit evidence, together with the victim's blood test revealing Rohypnol, was enough to get the creep the minimum sentence.

And within a matter of months after getting out, he was living in Boone County and hanging out with Garrett Pugh, Ashley's boyfriend's brother. This was one game of Six Degrees of Separation Bishop could do without.

"What are you doing here?"

Bishop's gaze shifted from the report in his hand to a pair of starched and ironed black jeans in front of him. Tipping his neck back, his eyes locked with the flashing green of Cassie's. Beneath the harsh fluorescent lights, a smattering of freckles across her nose stood out starkly against her pale skin.

"Is there a reason I'm not supposed to be here?"

Her lips pursed in tandem with her narrowing eyes. "I just don't want you to get in the habit of asking me to help you break the law."

"Me? Never." Bishop flashed her an offended look. "Besides, I really don't need your help, Sheriff. I just came by to pick up the rap sheet on a suspect related to my missing niece."

"You got Garrett Pugh's criminal record?" Cassie scoffed. "I could have given you that off the top of my head."

"Nope. Not Garrett Pugh."

"Who then?"

"Kevin Palmer."

"Who on earth is Kevin Palmer?"

"He's the owner of the vehicle parked in Garrett Pugh's driveway when I drove by after lunch."

Cassie crossed her arms. "You went back out to the Pugh house? If Garrett files a complaint that you're harassing him—"

"I told you, I just drove by."

"Then how do you know who owns a car in his driveway?"

Bishop flashed a cat-ate-the-canary grin.

"Tell me you didn't run his plates."

Maintaining his silence, Bishop just kept smiling.

"You know you're not supposed to—"

"Run plates on a vehicle that isn't directly involved in my investigation." He shrugged. "Turns out, this vehicle *is* involved in my investigation. So no harm, no foul."

As a red hue crept up Cassie's neck and colored her face with what could only be anger, Bishop stood.

"Bottom line, Sheriff, I'm going to do whatever's necessary to bring Ashley home safe and alive. In my line of work, the end justifies the means."

Without waiting for a reply, Bishop crossed the lobby and pushed through the front door. He looked back over his shoulder before descending the steps. Cassie faced him through the glass, arms at her sides, boots spread slightly apart. Like a beautiful gunslinger looking for a fight.

Chapter Seven

Cassie balanced the warm pie in one hand as she opened the front door to her family's ranch house, dreading tonight's conversation. Her brothers' voices rumbled out from the kitchen, a mixture of good-natured ribbing and laughter. Though she had her own place in town now and loved it, Cassie would always think of this ranch where she grew up as home.

"Finally! Hurry up. We're starving." Leave it to Nate to prioritize things.

Despite being fraternal twins, Nate and Noah couldn't be more different. Noah had planned from the get-go to join the sheriff's department and work with the rest of the family. Nate had seemed to want anything *but* a career in law enforcement. After wandering aimlessly for a few years, he'd come home for their father's funeral and decided to stay put. Hopefully, for good.

"Nice to see you, too." Cassie held out the dessert.

"You know I'm happy you're here." Nate gave

her a one-armed hug as he took the pie from her. "Apple?"

"Peach." Cassie followed him through the house to the kitchen.

"Hey, sis." Noah leaned against the butcher-block counter, a beer bottle in one hand.

"Hey. Where's Adam?"

"Out back, grilling steaks." Noah waggled his almost empty bottle. "Want one?"

"No, thanks." Cassie crouched in front of an antique washstand repurposed into a liquor cabinet and pulled out a bottle of tequila. "A day like today deserves shooters."

"I'll drink to that." Nate grabbed a lime from the fridge and sliced it into wedges. "Bad day at work?"

Cassie filled four shot glasses to the brim. "That's an understatement."

The twins whistled low in unison.

Without further ado, Cassie licked the back of her left hand between the thumb and forefinger and sprinkled it with salt. Picking up one of the glasses, she licked the salt, tossed the tequila and sucked on a wedge of lime. Her eyes closed, she exhaled as the burn slid through her, taking too little of the day's stress with it.

Adam came through the back door with a platter of steaming bone-in rib eyes and potatoes wrapped in foil. "Glad you made it in time for dinner." His smile, aimed at Cassie, dimmed when he caught sight of the empty shot glass in her hand. "Or am I?"

In response, she poured herself another and carried it, along with Adam's, into the dining room.

"Why do I get the feeling you're gonna ruin our appetites?" Noah joined them.

"Nothing ruins *your* appetite." Nate sat next to his twin. "And more pie for me if y'all aren't hungry for dessert."

Adam set the platter in the middle of the table, next to a basket of rolls. "Pie?"

"I swung by Marge's on my way here. My contribution to the feast."

"You really should learn how to bake one of these days. Or at least some basic cooking," Adam said. "'Cause unless you marry a chef, your kids are gonna be malnourished."

Cassie snorted. "Don't hold your breath. I had enough rug-rat-raising with you three."

"What are you talking about? I was a perfect child." Noah grinned. "But I'm good with you bringing professionally made stuff."

"I'm with Noah." Nate scoffed at his siblings' raised eyebrows. "*Not* about you being perfect." He pointed his fork at his brother, then swung it in his sister's direction. "But I'm still traumatized from your cooking when we were kids. Sure glad Adam took over when he was old enough."

Cassie tipped her head in acknowledgment, glad for the pleasant family banter. She'd be ruining it soon enough. "I agree. Why waste time learning something I don't enjoy when there are others who excel at it?"

"You *could* use a hobby." Adam passed the platter to Cassie. "Even Dad went fishing on his days off. You don't seem to do anything but work."

An image of her backyard shed turned pottery studio popped into Cassie's mind. Transforming lumps of clay calmed her mind when stressed. Soothed her soul while grieving. Connected her to a part of herself she kept hidden from everyone, especially her family. It was a part that came directly from her mother, the free-spirited artistic part that had destroyed her parents' marriage.

"Maybe that private investigator could be your new hobby." Noah talked around a mouthful of meat. "Spent most of the day with him, didn't you?"

Adam eyed Cassie. "What private investigator?"

"Just some PI from Houston, looking for his niece." Cassie focused on topping her potato with sour cream and bacon.

"Better grab him while he's in town, sis. He's a lot better-looking than most of your exes." Noah chuckled.

"I hadn't noticed." She shoved a bite of roll in her mouth, avoiding her brothers' eyes.

Noah snorted. "Come on, sis. Even *I* noticed."

"I'm *not* interested in him. Can we please change

the subject?" Not that changing the subject would help clear Bishop's pretty face from her mind.

"But what if he can cook?" Nate grinned at her from across the table.

"If he can, it wouldn't be anything I'd want to eat. He doesn't eat anything fried. Or *cow*. Marge had to make him grilled fish for lunch, and he ate his salad naked."

Noah's face transformed into the definition of horrified. "Where's he from?"

"Believe it or not, Texas. Born and bred."

Noah shook his head slowly. "That's just wrong." Then, as if proving his point, he shoved a chunk of medium-rare into his mouth.

Conversation waned as they all got serious about the food. Knives and forks clattered against plates, jaws chomped meat, Noah gnawed at his steak's bone. The Reed family was never one to stand on ceremony.

Even so, Cassie loved her brothers something fierce. How someone could think any of these three gold-hearted boneheads could turn rat, she had no idea. And as hard as Adam and Noah worked for her every day, Cassie dreaded bringing up the dire direction the trafficking case was taking.

As if reading her mind, Adam spoke first. "So, you want to tell us what's going on with the Rangers?" Setting his knife and fork down, he leaned back in his chair.

"And why can't we get into the files?" Noah asked.

A bite of blood-rare steak halfway to her mouth, Cassie paused. "Y'all know, huh?"

Adam nodded, his early humor gone. "But we wanted to give you a moment before we brought it up. Especially with you doing shooters."

"We also wanted you to eat something. No one likes a hangry Cassie." Noah's smile was a bit forced this time, but she loved him all the more for it.

There had never been any question that Cassie would take over when their father died. None of the male bravado hogwash that most women in her position would've faced. Because her brothers knew her to be the best candidate. Knew her drive and conviction for justice that had nothing to do with whether she was a man or a woman. They respected her. And more importantly, even at times like this when she had to be sheriff before sister, they loved her.

Cassie put her fork down and sat up straighter, doing her brothers the courtesy of looking each one in the eye before starting. "The Rangers informed me that they know about the leak. They think it's someone in our office."

Adam nodded, as if he'd already thought of the possibility. "No way the leak wears a badge, if that's what they're implying." He bit the side of his lip, apparently contemplating his next words. "Dave's the only possibility, and only because he's still pretty new and we don't know much about him—"

"Other than he's a pain in the butt," Noah chimed in.

"Other than that," Adam agreed, his tone more serious than jovial. "But the guy is all talk. On calls, he shies away from confronting anyone."

Excitement lit Noah's face. "Maybe that's it. He's trying to impress people when he's out drinking by exaggerating his involvement in cases."

Cassie waited and listened. She may be sheriff, but Adam and Noah were both excellent deputies. And although Nate didn't wear a badge, his intelligent observations offered a different point of view. She'd be shortsighted not to consider more ideas than just her own.

"I guess it's possible," Adam agreed. "But my money's on someone who's not a deputy."

"Can't be Heather in the county clerk's office," Noah said around a mouthful of roll. "She's too stupid."

"Noah!" Cassie had taught him better than that.

He looked at his sister and shrugged. "It's true, though. I mean, she's efficient enough, but have you ever tried to have a conversation with her? She's not the sharpest tool in the shed."

Cassie gave him the look that, as a child, had worked better than a scolding.

"Come on, sis." Noah flashed her the puppy-dog eyes that had also worked well when they were kids. "It's not like we're going to say this to her face."

"Doesn't matter." Cassie huffed, annoyed that her voice lacked the sharp tone she needed when faced with his faux-innocent expression. "No need to be so blunt about it."

"What about Judge Harmon's file clerk? I think her name's Mandy." Adam rose and paced around the table. "She sees all his paperwork, including requests for warrants."

"What about his secretary? She *prepares* all his paperwork." Noah leaned back in his chair.

"I've seen Mandy hanging out at the Dead End. She gets pretty wild after a few drinks." Adam stopped circling them. "Some biker jerk picks her up after work. Has long greasy hair and wears one of those military helmets. Tats all over his arms and neck."

"What makes him a jerk?" Nate asked, the only Reed still eating.

"He sits outside the back door and revs the engine while he's waiting for her."

Noah straightened. "I've seen that dude in the Dead End. Playing pool with another guy who had a bunch of tattoos. It was weird, 'cause they both had the same tat on their left hand."

"You got close enough to examine their tattoos?" Nate snorted. "What were you doing, trying to—"

"They were both bridging their cue sticks with that hand, wise guy." Noah sneered at his twin. "It was kind of hard to miss, even from a distance. Didn't get a good enough look at precisely what the tats were, though."

Cassie put both hands on the table and leaned forward, looking to wind them back down. "I appreciate the theories, but right now the Rangers are certain it *is* someone wearing a badge. They said there would be a thorough investigation of our department, and until they complete it we're off the trafficking case."

Noah rose so suddenly his chair fell over behind him. "Are you kidding? They're going to be working it instead?"

Cassie gritted her teeth. "Apparently not. They seem to be focused only on the leak."

"That's great." Picking up his chair, Noah sat again. "So they're just going to let the real bad guys run free and mess with innocent girls' lives because they think someone with a badge is leaking info." He snorted so hard he coughed. "Real heroes, those guys."

Cassie glanced at Adam. His eyes bored into hers as if he was sussing out additional information she hadn't delivered yet.

Steeling herself for the difficult part still to come, Cassie took a deep breath. "What I'm about to tell you stays between us. Understood?" She waited for their nods before continuing. "Right before I left tonight, Helen came into my office. She told me the Rangers asked her for copies of personnel reports."

"Well, obviously if they're investigating your department, they need those. Right?" Nate glanced from Cassie to Adam. "Right?"

"The only reports they wanted were mine, yours—" she looked at Adam "—yours—" her gaze moved on to Noah "—Lonnie's and Dad's."

"What the…?" Noah's brows pinched together. "Dad's? That makes no sense."

Adam stilled, staring at Cassie as if wordlessly communicating with her. When he got like this, he reminded her of the duck joke. Calm on the surface but paddling like crazy below. "Why isn't Lonnie here tonight? He needs to know this, too."

"I invited him. He said he had other plans that he couldn't change."

"Probably a poker game or a hot date." Noah scoffed. "That guy has perfected bachelor life."

"If you'd told him what tonight was about, he would have changed his plans." Nate glanced at her. They all considered Lonnie another brother, but Nate was especially close to his cousin.

"I told him it was important and he needed to be here." Cassie shrugged. "It was his choice. Don't worry, I'll make sure he knows."

Adam leaned forward, his forearms on the table. "So…why do they think *we're* involved?"

"Someone had to have fed them false info."

Cassie rubbed her eyes. "What we need to figure out is *who* and *why*."

"And in the meantime, no one's working the case." Adam blew out a hard breath.

"I bet Helen hasn't been locked out of the computer files," Nate said. "If one of you gave her a thumb drive, she could download them for you."

"That way, we could keep working on them from home." Noah's voice rose with enthusiasm.

"Working a case we've been pulled off of goes against protocol." Were her brothers seriously suggesting this? And here she'd been silently praising them for being such good law enforcement officers. "Plus, it could cost all of us our jobs, along with Helen."

"Only if we get caught." Noah pushed his plate away from him. "How many more girls are those creeps going to hurt or kill while we're sitting here twiddling our thumbs?"

Adam rubbed the back of his neck, avoiding her eyes. "Sometimes the end justifies the means, Cass."

There it was. The same phrase Bishop had used earlier, and she'd accused him of being an unprincipled scoundrel. Now her brothers were considering similar actions. She rose and reached for the tequila, pausing after she poured herself another shot.

She couldn't fault them for wanting to take ac-tion. That's what made them good deputies. But she refused to let them go about it the wrong way.

"I understand your frustration. I'm frustrated, too." She looked each of them in the eye. "But we're not resorting to unethical methods just because we don't like the situation."

"You don't have to. But Adam and I—"

"Noah, I said no. And don't forget, I'm not just your sister. I'm your boss." She drained her shot glass and stood. "You go rogue on this, you won't have to worry about the Rangers. I'll fire you myself."

Chapter Eight

Bishop had left the justice center intent on finding and staking out Kevin Palmer's house overnight. But exhaustion from the long day had caught up with him when he stopped by his motel room for protein bars and water. Though anxious to find Ashley, he'd reluctantly admitted that sleep would help him be sharper when he did confront Palmer.

Bishop headed out early the next morning, well rested and loaded for bear. As he drove west, the vivid oranges and pinks in his rearview mirror reminded him of the rainbow sherbet he'd loved as a kid. He rarely got to appreciate sunrises these days. The tall buildings where he lived blocked the view, and if he was already on the road, the notorious Houston traffic held all his attention.

The house he'd shared with his ex had a clear view to the east, and he'd watched the sun creep over the horizon while enjoying his first cup of coffee every morning. But after he quit the force and she kicked him out, he'd lost that view along with pretty much everything else.

Stopped at a railroad crossing, Bishop took a sip of his green smoothie. Buying a new blender yesterday had been worth it. When he'd asked the grocery clerk if they carried organic kale, the look on the kid's face had been priceless. The teenager had directed him to a frozen aisle for "them exotic foods." Despite the odds, he'd found bags of frozen, chopped, organic kale.

The last railcar, covered in talented graffiti, flew past and the crossing arms swung up. Bishop bumped across the tracks and worked his way west on a network of back roads.

His healthy lifestyle was just one piece of the new and improved Bishop. Anger management classes had also helped him come a long way from the walking time bomb he'd once been. He became acquainted with yoga and meditation as paths to find inner peace. He quit drinking and began purifying his body with antioxidants. He interned for a buddy's PI agency to see if going private was a good match for him. And that was when the ex kicked him to the curb. Apparently, living with an out-of-work detective who was trying to find himself was not what she'd signed up for. And to be fair, it *was* her house.

It took less time than expected to reach Flowertop, a town even smaller than Resolute. Bishop cruised down the main drag, where shop owners went about the business of opening up for the day. A middle-aged man, sporting horn-rimmed glasses—the same style that Bishop's grandfather had worn—twisted a rod to raise awnings above a five-and-dime store. A few doors down, a squat, round woman wearing a white apron over a red dress swept the sidewalk in front of a bakery. With her curly white hair, it was a safe bet she played Mrs. Claus in December.

The scent of warm dough and sugar crept into his truck like an invisible finger beckoning him. These days he avoided sugar, but he couldn't deny that the smell of freshly glazed doughnuts and cinnamon rolls could still tempt him. He grabbed his travel mug and took another swig of pulverized kale, fruit and protein powder—a taste he'd actually come to like.

He followed his GPS to the address he had for Palmer, a small, shabby house with a postage-stamp yard on the outskirts of town. The Boone County property records showed the house on Shady Oak Street was owned by a Norma Winston. Further searching revealed no link between Winston and Palmer. Not knowing if Palmer was flopping on a friend's couch or hiding out with criminals, Bishop intended to be cautious.

He drove past the address and continued down the length of Shady Oak. Lights were on in several houses. A man who looked to be about Bishop's age balanced his coffee tumbler and white hard hat while he unlocked his pickup. No sounds of kids playing outside yet. They were probably still watching cartoons in their pajamas.

Bishop turned right at the corner, a large rottweiler inside the yard's chain-link fence keeping pace with his truck, saliva flying with every bark. Looping into the alley behind the row of houses, he eased along until he was behind Palmer's one-car detached garage. He shifted into Park and hopped out to peek through the garage's side window, confirming the Corolla was inside.

Leaving the alley, he returned to Shady Oak and parked on the other side of the street, several houses down from Palmer's. From this vantage point he had a clear view of the front door, as well as a corner of the garage. With any luck, Palmer would come out of his hole and lead him to Ashley. If not, Bishop would make his own luck with the creep.

He opened his truck windows, hoping for some cross-ventilation. The late-summer temperature was already creeping up from the mid-eighties, the humid early morning air heavy and still. Even a slight breeze would be welcome as he settled in for a little sweaty reconnaissance work.

As a detective, he'd passed time on stakeouts drinking coffee and eating junk food. These days he turned to mindfulness. Thankfully, the neighborhood cooperated, providing quiet now that the rottweiler had calmed down. Bishop straightened his spine and got as comfortable as a six-foot man could get inside the confines of his truck. He focused his awareness on the sensations of his physical body, allowing thoughts to drift through his mind without judgment. But once his focus shifted inward, his chakras spoke to him.

Chakras, the body's seven main energy centers, needed to remain open and aligned for physical and emotional well-being. Bishop began with the first, or root, chakra. It was open. Next, the sacral chakra, connected to pleasure and sexuality—and just like that, his calming thoughts vanished as images of the contrary sheriff poured into his mind. Her tight ponytail swishing back and forth with the sway of her walk. Her slender body, its curves filling out her starched shirt and creased jeans. But more than her physical appearance drew Bishop to her. Her admirable, yet frustrating, integrity. Her compassion the previous day when he'd thought Ashley might be their Jane Doe. Her obvious affection for her younger brother.

Yep, Cassie was seriously messing with his sacral chakra. He'd wanted her from their first awkward conversation, and that desire just kept growing. He wanted the by-the-book sheriff naked except for a red-tape bow of justice wrapped around her. But he also wanted something more. Something intangible. Something he couldn't put a name to just yet.

Bishop pushed images of Cassie from his mind. He might not be bingeing on sugar-filled treats or gallons of coffee like he had when he was on the force. But allowing his attention to drift from his target for any reason wasn't just unhealthy, it was dangerous. Bishop refocused on Palmer's house.

THE MORNING AFTER the family dinner, Cassie tried to stifle a yawn as she parked in front of the justice center. Although not a morning person, she'd never been so much as a minute late to work. But today she'd crawled out of bed an hour before sunrise, aiming to beat the Rangers to the office. Giving in to the yawn, she leaned against the headrest and closed her eyes—just for a minute.

Loud rapping against the driver's-side window made her jump in her seat, her eyes jerking open. Texas Ranger Ward's wide knuckles continued to strike the glass until she rolled it down.

"Mornin', Sheriff." Mills stood next to Ward, an apologetic smile on his face.

Cassie sighed, her heart still pounding from being startled. "Morning, Ranger Mills. Beautiful day."

"It is indeed." Mills tipped his hat toward her, then followed his partner up the front steps.

Ward yanked on the building's locked door handle. "What time y'all open this place up?" he hollered at her.

Cassie ignored him. He had to have already known the door was locked. Otherwise he wouldn't have scared the bejesus out of her by knocking on her window. If he wanted to start his day with a hissy fit, fine by her. She took her sweet time getting her laptop and grabbing the satchel she used for carrying case files home at night.

She locked her vehicle and climbed the stairs at a slow pace, enjoying Ward's impatience through her reflective sunglasses.

"We're going to need a key to the building if everyone who works here keeps bankers' hours."

Cassie looked at her watch instead of unlocking the door. "Not sure six in the morning qualifies as bankers' hours, Ranger Ward." She took off her sunglasses and arched a brow.

When he only glared at her, Cassie smiled, unlocked the door and held it open for the two men. Ward strode into the building and directly down the hall toward their office.

Mills reached above Cassie's head to grab the edge of the door. "Please. Ladies first."

"Well, well, well. Your mama did a good job raising a gentleman."

His smile was warm. "She tried her best."

Once inside, Cassie relocked the front door. "I understand travel doesn't agree with some people." She tipped her head in the direction Ward had gone. "You think he needs some roughage in his diet or something?"

Mills's laugh echoed through the empty lobby.

Cassie leaned a little closer to him and stage-whispered, "Seriously though, are you really as nice as you seem? Or did you lose the coin flip and have to play the good cop this time?"

Mills matched her volume level. "I'm always the good cop. Especially when I'm working with guys like him." Mills winked, then took off after Ward.

Cassie cocked her head to the side, frowning as she watched him walk away. Was he truly a good cop? Or just better at playing one than Ward? Better to be safe than sorry and assume it was the latter.

She continued to her office, shut her door and locked it. At this point, she had no idea who she could trust outside of her family.

She drummed her fingers on the desk blotter, contemplating what she was about to do. Her eyes slid to her locked top desk drawer where she kept the short stack of files on her father's murder. All practically memorized by now.

Ward and Mills had only warned her away from the human trafficking investigation. While Cassie's gut told her that the traffickers had ambushed and killed her father, there was no proof. Until an official link was made, she had no problem treating her dad's murder as a separate case. She was about to tread a very thin line in not-so-narrow cowboy boots. But she'd sworn to find his murderer, and she aimed to uphold that vow.

Cassie unlocked the drawer and grabbed the manila folder, slapping it down on her blotter.

Although positive that the killer was linked to,

if not part of, the trafficking ring, Cassie sat at her desk and reset her perception of the case to zero. Assuming anything about a crime at the get-go could cause tunnel vision, forcing the facts to fit the assumption. Never mind that the anonymous call her dad and Dave had responded to that day had been about a suspicious group of men dragging a young woman into a neighboring house. Forget that at the time, her dad had been sure he was onto whoever was tipping off the bad guys.

Sean and Pete had been first at the scene after her father was shot. She'd read their incident reports countless times already, but she started through them again, looking for that one elusive fact that would shed light on the truth. While she flipped pages with her left hand, her right lay fisted on her thigh, nails digging into her palm. Just enough pain to keep her emotionally detached from what she read.

Nothing new. Same reports, same facts. Dave and Dad went on a call following an anonymous tip on the trafficking case. When they arrived, the house appeared vacant. Dad had Dave skirt around back while he took point at the front. Next thing Dave knew, shots were fired and when he came back around to the front, Dad was down on the ground, riddled with bullets.

Though most of the initial shotgun blast through the door hit Dad in his vest, some of the scatter landed low, nicking his femoral artery. But that was followed with close range shots from a 9-millimeter that screamed assassination.

Cassie closed her eyes in frustration as her stomach growled in hunger.

She pushed back from her desk and scrubbed her hands down her face, personally wanting to erase the autopsy pictures from her mind, but professionally trying to hold on tight to each detail.

She blinked several times, unable to stop the moisture in her eyes from sliding down her cheeks. She could only do so much compartmentalizing.

Using her sleeve, she gave her cheeks a rough swipe. She was stronger than tears. She would find her father's killers and ensure *they* were the ones crying behind bars.

But first, carb load.

Chapter Nine

Cassie pushed through the front door of The Busy B, gave Marge a quick smile and headed for the last booth. First thing her dad had taught her. *Always sit with your back to the wall.* She set her satchel beside her on the bench.

Rachel, who worked the breakfast shift, stopped by Cassie's table with a glass of water and a mug of black coffee. "Mornin', Cassie."

"Thanks, Rach." Cassie picked up the mug and blew at the rising steam. "So, is Brad enjoying being a big brother yet?" The server's four-year-old had decided he didn't really like his new baby sister after all.

Rachel huffed. "Well, he *did* stop demanding we return her."

"Sounds like progress."

"Oh, yeah. Lots of progress." Dark circles under Rachel's eyes revealed her new-mother exhaustion. "Now he's insisting we exchange her."

"For a boy?" Cassie took a careful sip, willing

to risk a burned tongue for a desperately needed caffeine boost.

"For a dog."

Cassie almost spewed coffee across the table.

"Yeah, yeah. Easy for you to laugh. Come on over and babysit them one of these days. Then you'll understand."

Cassie already understood. She'd all but raised her brothers, even before their mother had left. Her mom's ability to get lost in her artistic endeavors had led to dinners of cold cereal and no clean clothes for school. Lifting her hands as if surrendering, Cassie said, "No thanks. Been there, done that, got three brothers to prove it."

Rachel pulled out her pad and pen, her mocking grin all but calling Cassie a chicken. "So, what'll it be?"

"Number three, over easy. Extra bacon, extra crispy. And a biscuit with gravy instead of toast."

"In other words, the Cassie Special," Rachel said, her grin genuine this time. "Juice?"

"Tall orange. Thanks."

"Comin' right up." Despite her fatigue, Rachel headed for the kitchen with a spring in her step. Motherhood apparently agreed with her.

Cassie's mind drifted away like the steam on her coffee, returning to her father's death, the Rangers' suspicions and the dead-in-the-water trafficking case.

When Marge appeared with plates of steaming food, Cassie straightened, trying to physically shake the lingering melancholy.

Marge set the plates on the table, then planted a fist on each hip, looking down at Cassie with a motherly frown. "You okay, hon? You look like death warmed over."

Cassie gave her a halfhearted smile. "I always look like this when I get up before dawn."

"Hmph. More like you're workin' too hard." Marge smiled as Rachel set down Cassie's juice and topped off her coffee. "Rachel hon, cover my tables for me while I sit a spell, will ya?"

"Sure thing, Marge."

"That girl's a keeper." Marge slid into the booth across from Cassie. "Watch. She'll bring me coffee without me even havin' to ask." She grunted as she swung her stocky legs under the table and got situated. "Now, then. What in tarnation are you doing here this dang early? When you walked in, I about had a heart attack. Thought the clock done broke and I was movin' slower than a herd of turtles."

"Ha ha." Cassie forked hash browns into her mouth and washed them down with coffee, regaining tight control of her emotions. "Things have taken an unexpected turn at the office."

As predicted, Rachel dropped off a hot mug on her way to take an order.

"I heard. Texas Rangers in town, huh?" Marge stirred cream and sugar into the coffee. "They have anything to do with your mood?"

"That's a definite yes." Cassie dived into her easy-over eggs.

Marge's all-knowing brows arched. "Not hungry, are you?"

"As a matter of fact, I'm starving." Breaking off a piece of bacon, Cassie popped it into her mouth. "Or maybe I'm just eating my emotions."

"Or maybe you're hungry for a little down-home country justice."

Marge always jumped right to the heart of whatever had Cassie tied up in knots. "Maybe."

"Why don't you take a breather from stuffing your face and tell me what's really going on?" Marge invited confidence by leaning forward and resting her forearms on the table. "I swear on Doc's grave I won't tell a soul."

"Doc's not dead, Marge."

"I know that, sweetie. But I already paid for his plot in the cemetery and believe you me, it cost a pretty penny. So I'm still swearing on it."

Marge had her own rules of logic, and Cassie had never been able to convince her that some of them didn't make sense.

"It's not really a secret." She took a sip of orange juice. "The Rangers are taking over the human trafficking case. Kicked the whole department off of it." Cassie stabbed at her plate, loading her fork with another mouthful of food. "Losing that case sure sticks in my craw."

"Did they say why?"

The whole town knew about the trafficking ring to some degree. But Cassie couldn't tell Marge about the leak. Instead, she pivoted. "I'm going to concentrate on Dad's death instead."

Marge pursed her lips and nodded. "That explains the sad look on your face, sweetie. Working on your own daddy's murder." Marge sipped her coffee. "But didn't you say you thought them traffickers killed him?"

"I'd bet my badge on it."

"And didn't you just say them Rangers told you not to work that particular case?"

"*Technically*, no one knows who shot Dad, so *technically* Dad's case isn't related to the traffickers. Not officially, anyway. Therefore, I'm not working the case I've been booted off of. *Technically*." She lifted her shoulders in a shrug. "Not my fault if the two cases just happen to intersect."

Marge cackled. "Well, well, well. Never thought I'd see the day when you'd find a way around a direct order. Better be careful. Next thing we know, you'll throw caution to the wind and race down Main Street goin' thirty-two instead of the posted thirty."

"Very funny." Cassie fought the urge to remind Marge the town's speed limit was twenty-five, not thirty. "I just need to figure out how all the moving pieces fit together."

Marge aimed a sly smile at her. "Maybe your PI friend can help you figure it out."

Cassie choked on her hash browns. "Don't even start with me about that man."

"And why not? He might be useful, especially with him being an outsider. He might notice things you'd miss, seeing as you're so close to the situation and all."

Fair point.

"And sweetie, don't even pretend you haven't noticed how mighty fine that man is." Marge's sly grin returned.

Cassie groaned. "Looks aren't everything. He thinks he can do whatever he wants with no repercussions. Working with him, especially now with the Rangers in town, could spell disaster for my career."

"And you know all this just by spending a few hours with him yesterday?"

Cassie narrowed her eyes at Marge, for all the good it did. "The few hours yesterday were more than enough." She nibbled on a slice of bacon. "You don't understand. When he asked me to help with his case, it was the unethical, if not downright illegal, kind of help. And later he admitted doing something…well, something he shouldn't have. He's a loose cannon at a time when I can't afford any slipups. There's too much at stake. I have no intention of spending any more time with Mr. Bishop."

"You're being too harsh in your judgment of

him." Marge settled her rear end more firmly into the vinyl cushion. "And I'm fixin' to tell you why."

Cassie inhaled a deep breath and reined in her irritation. Like Helen, Marge had been there for every high and low point in her life since Cassie's mother abandoned the family. The two older women got along together about as well as oil and water, but they each loved Cassie in their own way.

"What you're forgetting is that he isn't here for some random case," Marge said. "It's about his flesh and blood. One look at that man's eyes and you can see he's worried sick about that niece of his. And you know darn well that people don't always color inside the lines when their loved ones are in jeopardy."

Cassie's gaze dropped to her plate. She did admire the PI's determination when it came to Ashley. Like a dog with a bone, he wouldn't stop searching until he laid eyes on her himself, despite no evidence of foul play.

And she couldn't argue Marge's point, because she couldn't tell her about the jeopardy her whole family was in right now. Sharing that information was a line Cassie refused to step over. Just as "coloring outside the lines" to save her family would never happen.

"Besides which, someone like your Mr. Bishop might help balance out your..." Marge paused, apparently fishing for the right word.

"There is no part of me that needs balancing

out." Cassie broke off a piece of biscuit with her fingers, dragged it through the creamy gravy, and topped it with a tiny bit of bacon. "And he's not *my* Mr. Bishop. You know I love you, Marge. But this conversation is over." She shoved the lump of carbs and fat into her mouth and chewed, not caring if she resembled a chipmunk with cheeks full of nuts.

Shaking her head, Marge slid to the edge of the seat and heaved herself up with a groan. "Suit yourself. Maybe I'll mosey on over to Doc's after closing and check on Mr. Bishop myself. Make sure he's all settled in, nice and comfy." She winked. "If you know what I mean."

Cassie's eyes widened. "He's at Doc's?" she mumbled, her mouth still full. Not that she cared where he stayed or if he was comfy. Just professional curiosity. Came with the badge.

"I didn't quite understand that, but I *think* you asked if he was staying at Doc's." Marge turned away before Cassie could nod. Over her shoulder she added, "Maybe you should just figure that out yourself with your own mighty detecting skills," then trundled off toward the counter.

"I don't really care," Cassie called after her. Who was she kidding? That aggravating man had gotten under her skin, and Marge knew it.

She pushed her plate across the table, her mind on Bishop. No doubt about it, he was a fly-by-the-seat-of-his-pants kind of guy who had no problem skirting the law if it suited his purpose.

Cassie yanked out her scrunchie and snapped it around her wrist, shaking her hair loose. Either her ponytail was too tight, or mental images of Bishop had brought her to the brink of a feverish headache. *Has to be the ponytail.* No low-principled private investigator could make the breath in her chest hitch and the pulse in her neck throb.

She massaged her temples, willing away all thoughts of Bishop. But as they left, her father's case rolled back in. She'd go home and review the files again. Figure out what the next step would be in solving his murder. And when she found his killer, there'd be more hell to pay than the devil even owned.

Chapter Ten

Stakeouts sucked, and mindfulness only took a man so far. After sitting for two hours waiting for Palmer to leave the house, Bishop's smoothie was gone and he'd exhausted all of his Cassie fantasies.

He climbed out of his truck to stretch his legs, his mind turning to Ashley. Her first dance recital at age four. The crisp fall afternoon when he'd joined Bob and Beth to help teach her how to ride a bike. Her fourteenth birthday, when he'd given her the silver turtle necklace, but then also surprised her with a trip to the gun range. The girl was a natural. Luckily, Beth had still been alive then. She'd been the one to convince Bob their daughter should learn how to handle guns safely.

Ashley wasn't perfect. Sometimes moody, other times sulky. What teenager didn't go through those growing pains? But she was a good kid, and he cursed himself again for ever letting Monique block his involvement in Ashley's life. Never again.

I'm coming for you, Little Turtle.

Time for a face-to-face with Palmer. And just

let the weasel try something, because right about now Bishop had a powerful urge to forget about anger management and issue a good old-fashioned beatdown.

He pulled on a chambray shirt and let it hang unbuttoned to cover the gun in the back waistband of his jeans, crossed the street and jabbed the doorbell. After pounding on the door brought no response, Bishop rang the bell again until even he was irritated by it.

He walked along the right side of the house toward the backyard, stopped by a six-foot chain-link fence with a padlock. Grabbing the top with both hands, Bishop stuck the toe of his boot into one of the fence's diamond-shaped holes and hoisted himself up and over. He dropped to the ground and paused, listening for any hint of life.

The silence held.

Staying tight against the side of the house, he crept toward the backyard. A quick peek around the corner revealed nothing but a solitary lawn chair on the patio, surrounded by cigarette butts. His gun in one hand, Bishop moved toward the back door.

Movement to his left caught his attention. He froze.

There it was again. A curtain fluttered against a window. He flattened himself against the back wall, the familiar rush of adrenaline sharpening his senses, readying him.

He leaned away from the house just enough for quick glimpse through the window. The curtains noved with a steady rhythm, pressing up against he glass, then falling away. Not the furtive movement of someone peeking out.

A deep breath, then Bishop spun, gun at the eady. The half-closed curtains continued to swing. Through the gap in the fabric, he spotted an oscilating fan. Blowing out the breath he'd been holding, Bishop lowered his gun. He peered through the irty glass. A bedroom, clothes all over the floor nd piled high on the bed.

No Palmer.

He continued on to the back door. Confirming was locked, Bishop made quick work with his ck picks. He pocketed the tools, donned a pair of itrile gloves and pulled his gun again before easng the door open. Sticking his head in, he looked oth ways. Empty. Remnants of food in takeout ontainers and pizza boxes filled the kitchen with au de garbage dump. Bishop approached an entryway to another room and paused. A sound beind him. *There it was again.* Trying to pinpoint , he returned to the stove. Two cockroaches had llen into a burner pan and were skittering in cirles, hissing at each other.

Back to the entryway. Keeping tight against the all, Bishop held his gun in both hands, aimed t the ceiling. He swung into the next room in a rouch, gun pointed toward the wall to his right,

then swinging it to the left. The sparse living roor
had nothing but two threadbare recliners and a T'
sitting on the floor.

With no other rooms to his right, he moved wit
stealth toward the side of the house he'd peeke
into. Four closed doors off a short hallway. The firs
one he opened was a linen closet, its shelves empty
Closing that door, he froze as a squeak sounde
somewhere in the house. He glanced up. A craw
space entry, covered with white plywood. Anothe
squeak. Not from above him.

He moved to the next door. Turned the kno
and pushed it open, his gun aimed into a smal
bathroom. It smelled worse than the kitchen. Flie
swarmed around the disgusting toilet, and Bisho
gagged as he moved past it. He ripped aside th
shower curtain, revealing nothing more than
filthy tub.

Only two rooms left to clear. Palmer had to b
in one of them. Bishop's heart rate increased, an
he stopped, hand on the knob. He would normall
take a deep breath to slow his pulse, but the bath
room's fetid smell had followed him.

He pushed the door open. A different stenc
rolled over him and into the hall. Death, wit
undertones of unwashed laundry and rank bod
odor. A closet door hung open, no one in its depth
Bishop flipped the wall switch, and a bare bul
came on overhead. Clothes littered the floor, alon

with empty beer bottles and cans, and ashtrays overflowed with cigarette butts.

He picked his way across the floor, stepping between the clutter and trash. As Bishop approached the bed, the piles of clothes he'd seen through the window morphed into a body. The dark areas surrounding it transformed from shadows to sheets soaked with dark, drying blood.

The man lay faceup, his blank eyes staring at the ceiling. A gaping slash in his neck resembled a macabre smile. Based on the mug shots Bishop had seen, this was Palmer, and he cursed himself for not pursuing him the evening before.

On the nightstand, a tipped-over pill bottle's label read "oxycodone." The top drawer was partially open, and he pulled it the rest of the way. Inside, a bag of weed, more pill bottles and a gun Palmer hadn't gotten to in time.

Bishop slid the drawer back in to where it had been. He'd have to call Cassie, tell her what he'd found. When she and her team arrived, they wouldn't be happy if the scene was compromised. He still needed to check the last room, probably another bedroom, and the attic crawl space. There'd been no other noises; maybe the squeaks had been from rats.

Intent on exiting the room without stepping on anything, Bishop shifted his balance before turning back toward the door. The hair on the back of his neck stood on end. A whisper of movement flowed toward him. He spun, gun already aimed toward the intruder. A large man came at him, wearing black jeans, black shirt and a black ski mask over his face. Before Bishop could pull the trigger, the man lunged. Pushing Bishop's arm out, the man slammed it into the nightstand, and the gun flew against the wall.

Bishop wrenched his arm free and charged the stranger, driving him into the closet across the room. Using the wall behind him as leverage, the man kicked Bishop in his gut. Doubled over, Bishop slid across the floor as the man kept kicking him.

The kicking stopped. A blinding pain exploded in Bishop's head. A darkness, filled with unrelenting anguish, crept toward his brain. Erasing thoughts. Wiping out the light until only a pinpoint remained. Bishop grabbed on to that tiny bit of light. He couldn't let the darkness win. Ashley needed him. Ashley nee…

CONSCIOUSNESS RETURNED TO Bishop in agonizing fits and starts. Pain pounded from inside his skull, stopping only when the blackness regained control. He fought that dark layer each time it moved in, even as his brain screamed to let it carry away the pain.

Forcing his eyes open, he cringed when the staggering blaze of light attacked them like a thousand sharp needles. Bishop propped himself up on one arm, a wave of nausea crashing over him. His eyes still blurry, he had no idea how long he'd been out. He sat, then stood, gritting his teeth against the protests from both his head and his stomach. He didn't know if he was alone. If Ashley had been in that last bedroom, his failure to clear it had sealed her fate.

Finally on his feet, he gazed in confusion at the bloody knife in his hand. His *ungloved* hand. He checked the corner where his gun had landed, but it was gone. Bishop looked at the bed. Palmer was still there. Still dead, from a wound that most likely had been made with the knife he held. His attacker had done a sloppy job of trying to frame Bishop.

It was a sure sign Bishop was getting close. It couldn't be a coincidence that Palmer was dead less than twenty-four hours after visiting Garrett Pugh. Garrett was a link to Ashley. Ashley was still missing. Bishop grabbed on to the nightstand, vertigo pulling him sideways. He needed help.

He pulled out his phone and hit Cassie's speed dial. Yeah, he'd put her on speed dial. *So what?* He braced himself as her phone rang. She would yell at him, but oddly enough he was almost looking forward to tangling with the beguiling by-the-booker.

"I thought we were done, Mr. Bishop." She hadn't even waited for him to ID himself. Apparently, he was programmed in her phone, too. Well, well.

"No time for pleasantries, Sheriff. I'm in Flowertop. Palmer's last known address. You might want to send your CSI guys over. And the coroner. He's already smelling a bit ripe."

His head throbbed, but he actually smiled the whole time she laced into him.

LIGHTS FLASHING AND gas pedal stomped to the floor, Cassie drove west. Her fingers grasped the steering wheel in a white-knuckled death grip. She hoped they'd uncurl eventually, because as soon as she arrived at Palmer's house, she intended to wrap all ten of them around Bishop's neck.

She'd arrived home from The Busy B with her dad's case, thinking her mood couldn't get any worse. But she'd barely opened the files when her phone vibrated in her back pocket. Caller ID did nothing to improve her frame of mind, which went further downhill with Bishop's ramblings about Flowertop, Kevin Palmer's house, a dead body. The man just couldn't stop meddling where he didn't belong.

Cassie turned off the emergency lights and eased her foot off the gas as she approached the town limits of Flowertop. It, like Resolute and so many small towns in Boone County, couldn't afford its own police force. As the sheriff, she enforced the law for these towns as well as unincorporated areas of the county. Which was darn lucky for Bishop. If Flowertop had its own police department, he'd already be sitting in an eight-by-ten interview room.

Parking in front of Palmer's house, she had a clear view of Bishop in the backyard behind a chain-link gate. He sat on the ground, leaning against the trunk of a live oak, holding something on his head. Cassie blew out a breath of exasperation, stepped out of her SUV and slammed the door.

She strode through the gate, eyeing the padlock hanging open on the post, and stopped in front of the defiant PI. "How exactly did you get back there? And don't tell me that gate was unlocked when you arrived."

Bishop peered up at her, his eyes broadcasting pain. The rolled-up sleeves of his shirt revealed bruises on both arms.

"Let me see." Cassie lifted his hand, which was holding a bag of frozen french fries, from the top of his head. The wound wasn't hard to find. A large knot, covered with blood-matted hair. Her anger faded at the sight of his injuries. "What did he hit you with?"

Bishop shrugged. "I have a feeling he kicked me. There was a lot of that happening, and he was wearing steel-toed boots." He lifted up his T-shirt, exposing arc-shaped bruises across his abs. His *very impressive* abs.

"My guys are already on their way. Helen called the JP, and the forensic team should be here soon. But I didn't realize you needed an ambulance." Cassie pulled her phone out.

"I don't need an ambulance. It's just a little—" he struggled to stand, wincing "—bump." He sucked in air between his teeth.

When Cassie started to tap her phone, Bishop grabbed it from her hand. "I told you, I don't need an ambulance." She reached to take it back and he held it above his head. "Don't you think you should take a peek at the dead guy?" He directed her to a back window. "Probably easier to identify from out here when you know what you're looking for."

She peered through the glass, confirming there was indeed a body on the bed.

"Explain to me how you just *happened* to see this." Cassie referred to his earlier phone call, which had made him sound like an innocent passerby. Not that she'd believed it for a single second.

He motioned toward a small building in the alley. "His car is in the garage, so I figured he was still home. I parked on the street to watch the house, waiting for him to leave so I could follow him. He didn't, so eventually I rang the bell." Bishop donned an innocent expression. "When he didn't answer, and only out of the utmost desire to ascertain his well-being, I—"

"Cut the crap, Bishop." Cassie planted her hands on her hips. "Yesterday you were champing at the bit to blame this guy for your niece's disappearance, only because his car was at Garrett Pugh's house."

"Also because of his criminal history." Bishop's

half smile segued into a tight line beneath flaring nostrils. "And she has a name."

It took Cassie's brain a second to process his last few words, but they still made no sense. "What?"

His arms at his sides, Bishop's fingers curled into fists. "My niece. She has a name." The words fell from his mouth like abrasive grains of sand. *"Ashley."*

Cassie's hands slid off her hips, and she took a small step toward him but stopped when Bishop's eyes drilled into hers with the red-hot burn of a branding iron, his pain and fury palpable.

"I didn't mean to depersonalize her." She kicked herself mentally. "I mean, Ashley." Referring to victims by pronouns or descriptors often caused their loved ones agony, as if law enforcement didn't see them as real people. Even if Bishop was a PI, he came to Resolute as an uncle.

His glare never wavered, and Cassie continued to meet it, standing tall with a neutral expression. Her dad had taught her to never show weakness by looking away first, even when apologizing.

As Bishop's gaze finally softened, he looked down at his hands as if surprised to see them fisted. He straightened his fingers and stretched them a few times before glancing her way again. "Sorry. I, uh, didn't mean to go off like that."

The tension in Cassie's body trickled away but she remained still, gauging Bishop's change in demeanor. "No big deal. It's just that you're usually so even-tempered. But hey, at least you didn't start punching walls or smashing windows."

He started to rake the fingers of both hands through his hair, then flinched when he touched his goose egg. He dropped his arms and blew out a breath. "Yeah, I've got a pretty good handle on the physical part of it."

"Physical part of what?"

Bishop scoffed. "Obviously, I still have a few anger issues."

"They have classes for stuff like that." Cassie peered through the window at the body again. "You might want to check them out."

"Been there, done that." He screwed his lips to the side. "Shoulda seen me *before* the classes."

Cassie raised her brows. She avoided men with complications like wedding rings, arrest records and emotional issues. But dang if Bishop didn't pique her curiosity more every time she was around him.

"Okay, walk me through it from when you approached the house."

"Can I get another bag from the freezer first? The french fries have defrosted, but I think I saw some onion rings in there."

Cassie crossed her arms and tapped her boot. She sympathized with his pain, but she wanted the whole story before everyone arrived.

Bishop's mouth tipped up on one side. "Okay, okay. Figured it wouldn't hurt to ask." Then he gave her a full accounting, from hopping the fence to getting jumped from behind.

"So, you cleared the last bedroom after you regained consciousness? What was in there?"

"Two sets of bunk beds. That was about it." Bishop leaned against the side of the house, wiping sweat from his brow.

"You don't need that looked at, huh?"

"I'm *fine*." He glared at her. "What happens now?"

"Now we wait for the troops to arrive."

"You aren't going inside first?"

"I'm sure the scene's already been disturbed enough, what with your fight and all. No need to compromise it even more." She turned her head and inhaled fresh air. The funk of death and filth clung to Bishop like cheap perfume. "Let's go wait on the front porch. But walk behind me. You need a shower."

"Hmph."

Cassie couldn't force Bishop into an ambulance. But she did make him sit on the front porch steps so he wouldn't fall over, while she stood a few feet in front of him on the walkway. It was sheer luck the wind was blowing in the right direction.

The Rangers arrived before anyone else. *Of course they did.*

"Sheriff." Ward's gaze slid from Cassie to Bishop. "Who found the body?"

Cassie folded her arms across her chest. "Afternoon, Ranger. What brings you out here?"

"Heard there was a murder."

"I reported a death, not a murder." She lifted her chin. "Either way, this isn't your case."

"Might be connected."

"I'll let you know what I find after our investigation is complete." Cassie narrowed her eyes at Ward. Behind him, Mills headed for the backyard.

"Since we're already here, I think we'll hang around. Talk to the techs." His lips stretched into a thin smile that didn't reach his eyes. "See what's what, if you know what I mean."

Oh, I know exactly what you mean. The Rangers planned to muscle their way into every case her office caught. They weren't just *investigating* her family. They were planning on taking their badges.

"So, again, who found the body?" Ward stared hard at Bishop.

"I'll make sure you get a copy of my report." Cassie returned his forced smile. "As soon as I find time to write it up." She pushed past him and joined Lonnie and Pete on the lawn.

"Why's *he* here?" His voice full of contempt, Lonnie watched Ward walk toward the back of the house.

"I sure didn't invite him."

Pete headed toward the arriving forensic team, and Cassie stepped closer to her cousin. "These guys are getting involved in a lot more than the human trafficking ring."

"They can't take over a case unless you ask for their help." Lonnie tucked his thumbs into his belt. "Just ignore them. They'll be gone as soon as they realize the leaks didn't come from our department."

"I'm not so sure about that." She lowered her voice even more. "Do me a favor? Stick around, keep an eye and an ear on them for me. I'm working on Dad's murder and want to get back to it. Plus, not sure how much more I can take of Ward today."

"You got it. You still taking lead on this?" Lonnie tipped his head toward Palmer's house.

"For now."

Lonnie nodded. "Let me know if you want a second set of eyes on your dad's file."

Cassie gave her cousin's shoulder a firm pat and motioned Bishop over.

"Who's he?" Lonnie asked.

"A PI from Houston."

"What's he doing at the crime scene?"

"It's a long story." Cassie waited until Bishop reached them. "This is my cousin Lonnie. Lonnie, Tyler Bishop."

The two men shook hands. Cassie knew her cousin, and before Lonnie could start questioning him, Cassie steered Bishop toward her SUV.

"Get in." She unlocked the doors, and they climbed inside.

Bishop settled into the passenger seat. "Why are Texas Rangers here?"

Cassie stared ahead through the windshield, biting her cheek. "I'd like to talk to you about something."

"Okay. But can we turn on the AC first?" He dragged his shirt sleeve across his brow.

"Sorry." She pushed the ignition button and cranked up the air, her nostrils rebelling at the scent of decomp. "I don't mean talk now. Think you'll feel up to meeting tonight? *After* you've showered."

Bishop chuckled. "I told you, I'm fine. How 'bout I buy you dinner? Where's the closest sushi place?"

Cassie turned to face him. "I am not eating raw fish and seaweed."

He gave her a two-dimpled grin and a wink. *Heaven have mercy.* She wasn't even used to the dimples yet. But the wink *with* the dimples pushed her pulse to hummingbird rate times two. This man was going to be even more trouble than she'd expected.

"I'll meet you at The Busy B." *Keep it nice and casual.*

"Is that the only place in Resolute to eat?"

She cocked a brow at him. "You don't like the diner?"

"I *love* the diner." The exaggerated enthusiasm

in his voice told her otherwise. "But I was hoping for someplace with a bit more atmosphere."

Bishop wanted atmosphere, did he? For the first time all day, Cassie smiled. "I know the perfect place."

Chapter Eleven

Sitting in her parked SUV and watching Bishop over the top of her steering wheel, Cassie chuckled. The big bad PI stood next to his truck in the packed, crushed-rock parking lot, his mouth hanging open like a kid on his first trip to Disneyland. She figured a man from Houston would have seen at least one two-story neon sign blazing over a gigantic converted barn, but apparently not.

To be sure, the Resolute Chute was a unique and popular local landmark. The place served the best food in town—something she'd never admit in front of Marge—but at 9:00 p.m., the tables were pushed aside and the place turned into a boot-stompin', two-steppin' honky-tonk with live music.

As much as she enjoyed observing Bishop's undisguised show of amazement, not to mention his heart-stopping backside, she stepped from her SUV and self-consciously adjusted her soft teal shirt. With the top buttons open and the lapels falling away on either side, a disturbing amount of cleavage was exposed.

Marge had given her the shirt as a birthday present one year, assuring her she looked sexy, not like a hussy.

Well, sexy didn't come naturally to a gal raised in an all-male household. So she'd toned down her appearance by exchanging the black jeans she wore to work for a pair of broken-in blue ones. Her well-worn boots crunched against the gravel as she approached. "How do you like our little dance hall?"

"Little?" His head swiveled toward her, and he did a quick double take. His gaze turned intense, penetrating. "I guess it's true, the stars *do* shine bright deep in the heart of Texas."

A light breeze lifted her hair, hanging loose across her shoulders, but her cheeks still warmed at his wide eyes and parted lips. *Come on, Cassie, think of something to say.* Never at a loss for words before in her life, she just stood there like a statue, staring into Bishop's fathomless blue eyes.

"I've never seen you with your hair down." A smile tugged at Bishop's mouth as he took a step back, giving her a head-to-toe once-over. "You look…softer."

Oh, man. He walked right into that one. Fisting her hands on her hips, Cassie huffed with false indignation. "Are you saying I usually look hard?"

His smile vanished. "No, not at all."

She could practically hear the normally unflappable man slamming on the brakes.

"What I meant to say is that you look less... less severe."

She pursed her lips and tapped her boot.

"Okay, that's not right, either." He ran a hand through his hair. "Less serious? Maybe less professional?"

"Yes." Cassie nodded, still stifling her amusement. "A sheriff is *supposed* to look professional while at work."

He nodded with her, his shoulders relaxing. "Then let me start over. You look much less professional tonight." He flashed his dazzling smile, the same one he'd given Marge at The Busy B when he asked for his fish grilled, not fried. The one where his dimples took center stage. "Not what I was originally going for, but I hope you'll take the compliment in the spirit it was given."

"I will. Thank you." His obvious appreciation made fussing with her hair and makeup, as well as the ridiculous amount of time spent deciding how far down to unbutton her shirt before spritzing her throat with her favorite perfume, worth it.

His gaze raked over her in a slow move that made her glad for the lengthening shadows that masked her heated cheeks. "So, dinner *and* dancing?"

"You said you wanted atmosphere." Cassie gave him a self-satisfied grin before spreading her arms wide toward the building. "I give you atmosphere."

She led the way inside and through a vintage

wooden cattle chute that ended at a hostess stand. The petite brunette standing next to it was dressed like a rodeo queen.

Flashing a smile at Cassie, and a much bigger one at Bishop, she said, "Hey, Sheriff."

"Evenin', Crystal. How's your mama?"

"Doing just fine. Should be home from the hospital tomorrow."

"Glad to hear it. Tell her I said hey."

"I sure will. Y'all here for dinner, or just gettin' your drink on before the band starts?"

"I'm here for both." Cassie hooked a thumb in Bishop's direction. "Not sure about him."

Crystal's gaze lingered on Bishop like he was a juicy slab of meat. "This your first time here?"

"Yes, ma'am, it is."

"Well then, you're in for a real treat. We have the juiciest, most tender steaks in all of Texas." The barely-twenty-one-year-old licked her upper lip with the tip of her tongue. "And we make sure the customer always leaves satisfied."

Cassie rolled her eyes, but only in her mind. "It's just a darn shame he doesn't eat beef."

"Oh, I'm sure I'll find *something* delicious here to devour." Bishop gave Crystal a playful wink as he turned his eyes to Cassie. But there was nothing playful about the intense look they shared. It was hot. Smoldering hot. Cassie's mouth went dry, and the tempo of her heart jumped a notch or two.

Crystal led them to a small table near the dance

floor. "I'll seat y'all here, so you've got quick access when the dancin' starts." She set two menus on the table and headed back to her stand.

Bishop held Cassie's chair for her before taking his own seat. "This is quite a place."

"Disappointed that I didn't take you to one of those salad bars?"

"You have one of those here?" His eyebrows shot up in excitement.

"Of course we do. You just have to wait until the Webbs are sound asleep, then you hop the fence and nibble away at their vegetable garden." She bit her bottom lip to keep a straight face. "It's perfect for a man like you, who likes his salad *nekked*."

They both burst into laughter, setting the stage for an evening that Cassie looked forward to, despite the serious conversation she had planned.

Bishop twisted in his chair to get a view of the entire building inside. Cassie followed his line of sight as it moved from the crowded bar to the shuffleboard and pool tables to the souvenir stands geared to visiting tourists. Then he turned his blistering gaze back to her. "I thought they had live music."

Cassie gave him a pleasant smile, hoping it wasn't obvious how much his attention affected her. "That comes after dinner. With the dancing."

"I see. And…" He trailed off as his eyes latched on to something over her shoulder. Cassie turned, smiling to herself. Just past the far end of the dance floor, in a separate, good-sized pen surrounded by rail fencing, a mechanical bull bucked its current rider into the hay surrounding it.

Bishop shook his head. "I thought those things went out of style after *Urban Cowboy*."

"Don't worry. They've got mats under the hay. Long as you don't land on your neck funny, you'll be fine."

Bishop met Cassie's eyes. "What makes you think I'm getting on that thing?"

She gave a one-shoulder shrug. "Tradition. Everyone rides it their first time here."

"Well, how about we just keep the fact that it's my first visit on the down-low?"

Cassie picked up her menu, hiding her grin behind it. "Too late. Crystal asked, you answered. By now she'll have spread the word."

"Great. Just great." Bishop left his menu on the table. "They have anything *except* beef here?"

Reaching across the table, Cassie tapped on a section of entrées. "Their chicken is good. Crispy on the outside, juicy on the inside."

"Like *fried* crispy?"

She glanced up from beneath her lashes, then batted them at him. "Oh. That's right. You don't like cow *or* fried. Well, shoot. This place has the best atmosphere around, but I completely forgot about your list of won't-eat vittles." His fingers brushed the back of her hand, and a chill raced up her arm, leaving goose bumps in its wake. "They have really good shrimp," she said, trying to recover. "No, wait. That's fried, too. Dang it. Well, check the appetizers and sides." Ducking back behind her menu, she hid both her shocked reaction to his touch and her amusement with his food dilemma.

Several minutes later, a waiter approached their table with two waters. "Howdy, folks. My name is Mark and I'll be serving you tonight. Is this your first time visiting the Chute?"

Cassie grinned up at him. "You know it's not *my* first time, Mark."

"Sorry, Sheriff. You know we have to ask."

"Well, it's a good thing you did tonight." Cassie tipped her head toward Bishop.

"Oh, so this is *your* first time here?"

Bishop groaned.

Oblivious, Mark went on. "Well, sir, you're in for a real treat. Just so you know, we stop serving dinner at nine and push the tables aside, 'cause that's when we bring out the band and the dancing starts. Can I bring y'all anything else to drink while you look over the menus?"

"I'll have a Oaxaca old-fashioned. And I think we're ready to order." Cassie glanced at Bishop, one brow raised. He nodded and she continued. "I'll have the tomahawk steak, rare. Loaded baked potato, and blue cheese on the salad."

"Excellent choice." The waiter faced Bishop. "And for you?"

"Iced tea with lemon. *Un*sweet." He glanced back down at the menu. "I noticed you have a smothered chicken breast on the menu."

"Yes, sir. It's a very popular choice. In addition to the bacon, cheese, grilled onions and mushrooms, a lot of our customers add jalapeños."

Bishop nodded as if mulling it over. "I'll have the grilled chicken breast with just the vegetables on it."

The waiter paused, pen hovering in midair over his order pad. "Onions and mushrooms, hold the cheese *and* the bacon?"

"That's right." He closed the menu and shifted forward in his seat. "And toss the jalapeños on it, too. And I'd like the sweet potato, no toppings. Vinaigrette on the side for the salad." Bishop handed his menu to the waiter.

"Very good, sir." He picked up Cassie's menu. "I'll have those drinks right out." He hurried off toward the bar.

Cassie leaned toward Bishop, her forearms on the table. "Glad you found something that fits your rigid diet."

"Look who's talking about rigid." A smile tugged at Bishop's mouth. "I just like to live a healthy lifestyle."

She huffed, refusing to get into a discussion about her supposed inflexibility. She'd heard it enough from people she knew. And Bishop most certainly knew nothing about her. "I suppose you do all kinds of other weird woo-woo stuff, too."

Bishop's brows pulled together in puzzlement. "Woo-woo stuff?"

"Yeah, you know. Yoga. Meditation. Stuff like that."

"In what world are yoga and meditation considered woo-woo?"

"In this one right here." Cassie slapped a hand on the table. "Good old Texas."

"I live in Texas, too, remember? Maybe you just need to expand your horizons."

"So, you *do* do yoga and meditation."

"Yes, I do both of them. Usually every day. Especially meditation."

"Ooh. Can I watch sometime?" Cassie widened her eyes in mock excitement. "You know, *expand my horizons?*"

Bishop massaged his forehead. "Meditation isn't something you watch. It's something you do to re-center your chi. Your energy."

"Woo-woo." Cassie wiggled her fingers in the air.

The waiter brought their drinks, then scurried to the next table. Cassie took a sip and sighed with pleasure.

"What's that thing called?" He nodded toward her glass.

"Oaxaca old-fashioned." She took another sip before setting it down. "It's an old-fashioned, but with tequila, mescal and xocolatl bitters. Want a taste?"

He shook his head. "*What* kind of bitters?"

"Xocolatl. Chocolate mole bitters." She laughed at his grimace, then looked around at the mechanical bull. "Speaking of expanding horizons, it's about time for you to ride that bull. And I strongly recommend doing it *before* you eat. You'll thank me later."

"I may be from out of town, but I'm not naive. There's no way you're getting me on that bull." Bishop rested his forearms on the table and leaned forward. "Besides, the only people lining up to ride it are women."

"And here I thought you were a modern man with all that yoga, meditation and whatnot." Cassie mirrored his position. "Didn't think you'd play the macho card so soon."

He relaxed against the back of his chair. "Not playing the macho card, darlin'. I'm playing the bullsh…the bull card. There's no way all newcomers are expected to ride that thing."

"Nice save, Bishop."

Just then the manager, Sal, stopped by their table. "Sheriff, good to see you."

"Hey, Sal. How are things?"

"Busy, as always." Sal turned to Bishop. "And who's this? I don't remember seeing you at the Chute before."

"This is my, uh, friend, Bishop. He's just passing through." Cassie ignored Bishop's arched brow. Well, what did he expect her to call him? Colleague? Not a chance. Boyfriend? Laughable. Date? As if. Friend was as good as he'd get.

"Welcome, Bishop. Always good to see a new face." Sal winked at Cassie. "The regulars love the entertainment when a newcomer comes to the Chute." He pointed over to the mechanical bull. "When you go up there, just tell Rowdy I sent you. That'll get you to the front of the line. Don't want to interrupt your date any longer than necessary."

Cassie's satisfied grin slid off her face. "Wait, this isn't a—"

Bishop cut her off, eyeing the manager with suspicion. "So you're telling me all newcomers have to ride the bull?"

"Hasn't anyone told you?" Sal's glance swung to Cassie, then back. "It's tradition. Now go have some fun." He clasped Bishop on the shoulder and moved on to the next table.

Cassie's cheeks hurt from smiling. "Told ya."

"What happens if someone refuses to ride the bull?"

"Ooh, I wouldn't do that if I were you." Cassie shook her head from side to side. "That would make you a bad sport, and no one likes a bad sport."

"Not even my *date*?" Those dadgum dimples appeared again.

"I'm not your date." She crossed her arms. "Sal was just confused."

"How 'bout this?" Bishop leaned in again, this time like a conspirator. "I ride the bull if you call this our first date."

Cassie matched his low volume. "That would imply a second one in the future. Which is impossible, because this *isn't* a date."

"Have it your way." Bishop shrugged. "Then you're spending the evening with a bad sport. Doesn't say much for your taste in men, now does it?"

After staring at each other for a full minute, Cassie let out a groan of frustration. "Fine. This is our first date." *And there will never be a second.* "Now go ride that bull."

"A deal's a deal." Bishop slapped both hands on the table for emphasis and stood.

Cassie raised her glass toward Bishop. "By the way, his name is Old Horny."

Bishop looked over at the bull. "But he doesn't have horns."

She snickered. "That's not how he got his name."

Bishop watched the current rider, his brow furrowed in confusion. Cassie rolled her lips between her teeth to keep from laughing. How long would it take him to realize the girl riding the bull in a slow, sexy motion had a very satisfied smile on her face?

Bishop looked back at Cassie, a crooked smile parting his lips. "Ah, I get it. She does look very happy."

"I'll bet her date does, as well." Cassie chuckled.

"Good Old Horny is famous for putting people in the mood."

He glanced again at the bull. "Hmm. Maybe you should give him a ride, too." He winked at her and strolled off toward the bull.

"Maybe I should," she murmured, watching him walk away from her. "Maybe I should."

Bishop got in line behind the girls, but Rowdy motioned him up to the front. When the current rider swung one leg over the bull's back and slid off without falling, everyone watching her cheered. Cassie stretched her legs out under the table and got comfortable for the show.

Rowdy started with the slowest speed, and although Bishop should have looked ridiculous, Cassie's breaths came faster with each movement. Backward and forward. Bucking and swaying. The speed increased and Bishop held on with perfect form. The longer the ride, the more the bull twisted and changed directions. His left arm in the air for balance, Bishop still managed to stay centered. But as the pace picked up even more, his movements crossed over into slapstick.

Cassie's panting turned to laughter. Impressed that he'd held on this long, she cheered along with the crowd as his butt flew up off the seat and slammed down. His thighs lost their grip of the bull's sides and his arm swung wildly in the air. And still, Bishop refused to let go. A wild ride that would have tossed most anyone else to the ground long ago slowed to a stop. Sliding off Old Horny, he seemed surprised at the crowd's clapping and whooping. When he bowed with a flourish, diners and employees alike gave him a standing ovation.

Sal approached the table and Cassie slipped him the twenty she'd promised if he played along with the tradition story. "Here's another ten for Rowdy."

"Always happy to oblige, Sheriff." Sal retreated before Bishop reached the table.

Cassie noticed a slight limp before Bishop eased into his chair with a wince. "Got a little hitch in your git-along?" Not about to admit he'd crushed the ride, Cassie's lips twisted into a smirk.

"Guess I've been out of the saddle too long." He guzzled his iced tea. "How'd I do?"

"Not too shabby for a city boy." Sucking on an ice cube from her empty glass, she asked, "When you say 'out of the saddle,' would that be the grocery store horsey ride?"

"Cute. Very cute. And by the way, I know you set me up. I never figured such a stickler for the rules would orchestrate such a well-planned practical joke."

Hmm. The man was more observant than she gave him credit for. She widened her eyes. "I don't know—"

"Like he…heck you don't." Bishop's eyes twinkled with amusement. "I saw you handing Sal the cash."

Instead of denying it, Cassie doubled over with

laughter. "What can I say? It was worth every penny. Especially when you were flying every which way toward the end." The laughs tapered off and she wiped her eyes with her napkin. "Sorry. What were you saying about saddles?"

"I used to ride horses every day. I haven't had a chance to for a long time."

Cassie swallowed the sliver of ice, surprised by his words. "You live on a ranch?"

"Not now." Bishop nodded at some of the girls from the bull-riding line as they passed by on their way to the bar but kept his attention on Cassie. "But I grew up on one just outside of Houston. I rode almost before I could walk. My first job was riding fences. Seemed there was always a section to repair."

"Why'd you leave ranching?"

Bishop waited until their server refilled their water glasses. "Because I wanted to be a cop."

This guy had more layers than an onion. "But you didn't pass the exam, and decided to go private?"

"Oh, I passed the exam with flying colors." He smiled at her shocked expression. "After I'd put in my time on patrol, I took the detective's exam and passed that, too."

Embarrassment burned through Cassie, turning to indignation. "Why didn't you tell me that in the diner when I—"

"Said private dicks don't know as much as real

cops?" Bishop chuckled. "As I recall, you didn't give me a chance to answer before you stomped out of there."

Her face warm, Cassie intended to regain the upper hand. "Why were you fired?"

Bishop scoffed. "Good guess, but no, I wasn't fired."

Now he was just yanking her chain. Payback for the bull ride. "No one in their right mind quits a detective job to become a PI. That's a move retired cops make when they can't give up the game."

"Guess I'm not in my right mind, then." He sipped his disgusting, unsweet tea.

Cassie frowned. "It doesn't make sense. Why would you do that?"

Mark arrived with plates of food, and Bishop picked up his fork. "Well, darlin', that's a story for our next date."

CONSIDERING THE PLACE was a steakhouse, Bishop's meal exceeded his expectations. His chicken was surprisingly tender, the vegetables perfectly seasoned, the salad cold and crisp. Add lively dinner conversation, with Cassie pointing out interesting townsfolk and sharing humorous anecdotes about them, and the evening was shaping up to be perfect.

Perfect except for his constant worry about Ashley. It was a drumbeat that grew louder in the back of his mind with every passing moment. He had to eat and sleep, though, and he needed to form a bond with Cassie. If he played his cards right, she could help him more than she already had. It was a bonus that he genuinely liked her and wanted to get closer to her. Maybe after a few slow dances later, he'd have a chance to get to know her as well as everyone else around here seemed to.

After a busboy cleared the table, Cassie ordered pecan pie with whipped cream and a cup of coffee. Bishop declined, claiming he was full from dinner.

Cassie pursed her lips. "Come on. I ate more than you did, and I still have room. To complete the perfect food pyramid, you gotta start with alcohol and finish with dessert."

Bishop cringed inwardly, fighting the urge to lecture her on nutrition. There were more important things to discuss. Like Cassie's reason for this entire evening.

Mark returned with Cassie's pie and coffee and set the bill holder near Bishop. "I'll just leave this here for whenever you're ready." He took off at a fast clip, probably needing to finish with his tables before the dancing started.

Time to get the ball rolling. Bishop rested his arms on the table. "I've enjoyed tonight." He could swear his chakras aligned when Cassie's face lit up with a smile. "But it goes against my nature to stop searching for Ashley just so I can have a good time. I'm only here because you said we need to talk."

After one small bite of pie, Cassie put down her fork. "You're right. And that's what I want to discuss. Ashley. What's your next step in finding her?"

Immediately on guard, Bishop paused before answering. Was this an offer of help, or a trick to find out what he was up to? "Hard to say. I'm figuring it out as I go. Why?"

"I think it would benefit us both if we work together on our cases."

For a minute Bishop just stared, not expecting her offer. "What changed your mind?"

Cassie frowned. "Changed my mind?"

"You don't remember me asking you for help in the diner?"

"Working together doesn't mean I'm willing to break the law." Cassie's professional tone returned for the first time tonight. "I'm suggesting that an extra pair of eyes might catch something we've missed." She sighed, her voice softening again. "I *want* to help you find Ashley." She reached across the table and rested her hand on his.

The sincerity in her voice, the warmth in her touch, broke through Bishop's defenses. Since becoming a PI, he'd handled every case professionally, with no emotional involvement. But his search for Ashley was different. It was personal. It was eating him up on the inside, despite all attempts to maintain a Zen energy.

"I would appreciate your help." His voice cracked and he cleared his throat. "What case are *you* working on?"

Cassie pulled her hand back and sipped her coffee. "My father's murder. I've gone over the reports until my eyes bled. I was going through them again this morning, but was interrupted." The corner of her mouth twitched. "I had to respond to some bonehead's call to a murder scene."

Bishop shrugged. "Sorry about that. Figured you'd want to know."

"I did. But I still don't understand why you're so sure Palmer had anything to do with Ashley."

"He has a criminal record that includes sexual assault on a young woman. He gets out of jail and he's hanging out with Garrett. Ashley is at Garrett's house right before she disappears. Someone kills Palmer and tries to frame me while I'm there looking for Ashley. And then, Texas Rangers show up at Palmer's after he's murdered." He cocked his head. "What's that about, anyway?"

Cassie let out a long, slow breath as if trying to cool her temper. "The Rangers are here to investigate one of our cases that we've been working for the past couple years. My dad thought he was getting close to solving it when he was killed." She straightened in her chair. "Meanwhile, the Rangers have kicked my whole department off the case." Cassie picked at her uneaten pie with her fork. "That's why I'd like you to be the fresh eyes on Dad's murder."

"Why were they at Palmer's? Is he what they're investigating?"

Cassie's troubled gaze found his eyes. "No. They just showed up, claiming it might be related. But that's hogwash. They had no right to be there." A shadow crossed her face. "They seem intent on taking over *all* our cases."

"What case did they kick you off of?"

"There's a human trafficking pipeline running through Boone County. In fact, the Jane Doe we found right before you got here was one of their victims. We were all hands on deck to track them down, but the Rangers trumped our efforts."

Bishop jerked upright in his chair, his stomach tight with anger. The uncontrollable fury he'd thought vanquished spread through him like a malignant old friend, tensing every muscle until even his jaw ached. "You knew there were human traffickers here the whole time, and you never thought to mention this to me?"

Cassie's mouth dropped open, apparently shocked by his tone.

He slammed his hand on the table. "Ashley is eighteen, good-looking, and disappeared into thin air, and you didn't think this was pertinent information? You even checked your Jane Doe to make sure it wasn't my niece."

"Bishop." She spoke slowly, as if still surprised from his outburst. "It was a confidential investigation. And Garrett said—"

"Right." He scoffed. "You just accept some cock-and-bull story about her eloping, knowing at least one woman was dead because of a human trafficking ring." Bishop stood, fists clenched at his sides, glowering down at Cassie. "For all you know, Ashley could have been with your Jane Doe when she was killed. And because you just had to follow the rules, she could be halfway across the country by now."

"No." Cassie shook her head. "The timing doesn't track. I—"

"Save it." Bishop muttered a curse as he pulled out his wallet and slid five twenties into the bill holder. "The extra there is for the tip. If you want to keep drinking, buy your own." He stalked out of the building, not even trying to calm down. The old Bishop was slithering back in, ready to resume control. And the new Bishop was ready to let him.

WHAT THE... CASSIE watched Bishop's fine backside stalk out of sight, still in shock from his Jekyll-and-Hyde personality.

He hadn't even given her a chance to explain before he stormed out. *Fine.* He could find Ashley on his own.

Cassie waved over a waiter and ordered another drink. Mostly out of spite. She could pay for her own drinks, thank you very much, *Mister* Bishop.

After the scene he made, drawing the attention of everyone around them, Cassie seethed on the inside while keeping a smile on her face. *Everything's fine here, folks. Nothing to see. Move along.* She picked up her fresh drink, the telltale signs of her hard-fought control marking her palm. Four crescent-moon dents; only one drew blood. She set the glass back on the table.

She closed her eyes and took a deep breath. *Put yourself in Bishop's shoes.* If one of her brothers or Lonnie were missing, she'd be madder than a wet hen if someone withheld relevant information. And they were men trained to take care of themselves. Ashley was a teenager, out there on her own. Unless she eloped with Michael. *But what if she didn't?* Cassie's eyes popped open.

Having already paid for her drink, she dashed for the exit door. Bishop was probably already gone, but she knew where he lived. Almost mowing down a couple walking in, Cassie skidded to a stop in the parking lot. Bishop stood by his truck, his back to her. She inhaled a deep breath, exhaled and came up behind him.

"I understand, Bishop."

He turned around, his face still contorted by anger. "You understand *what*?"

"Why you're so mad at me. I would be, too."

He shook his head. "It's not just you I'm mad at. I never should have blown up at you like that." His shoulders slumped. "I feel like I'm losing control. Reverting back to who I used to be."

"I should have told you about the trafficking ring. But the timing still doesn't work for them to have grabbed Ashley here. They'd already left the stash house in Resolute."

"But even the slightest chance…" He turned pleading eyes on Cassie.

"If you'll let me, I'd still like to help you find her. Work together on our cases." She held her breath, willing him to agree.

"I can't do it unless you're going to be completely honest with me." Bishop folded his arms across his chest. "About everything."

Revealing the real reason the Rangers were in town, telling Bishop about the leak and the threat to her family, made her stomach hurt and her chest relax at the same time. It was confidential information she shouldn't share. But working together, Bishop might help her find the real person behind that leak. "Fine. But that goes for you, too."

"Deal. But don't tell me what I legally can and can't do."

Cassie gnawed her lower lip. Was she really going to agree to this? "All right. But don't ask me to do anything illegal. Or unethical. Or—"

"Okay, okay." His mouth kicked up at the corners. "When do we start?"

Chapter Twelve

In her dream the next morning, Cassie balanced on a wobbly step stool and stretched high to shut off her smoke alarm. As soon as she stepped down, it went off again. The cycle continued until she surfaced long enough to recognize her phone's ring. Fumbling it off her bedside table, she answered without opening her eyes.

"Sheriff Reed." Her head fell back on her pillow.

"Hey, Cass. It's Lonnie."

Bolting upright, Cassie forced her eyes open and looked at her phone. Half past nine. "Dang it. I overslept." *First time for everything.* She pressed the speaker button and got out of bed, tripping over the clothes on the floor. *Stupid teal shirt. Only ever wrangled me bad luck and worse judgment.* "Anything wrong?" She kicked the shirt across the room.

"Just thought I'd check on you. You were MIA yesterday until the Palmer thing, and when you didn't show up this morning, I was worried."

Cassie loved her independence, but she appreciated her cousin's concern, too. He was more like a brother anyway, growing up with her family after his dad kicked him out. "I don't care what anybody says about you, Lonnie. *I* love you."

His deep chuckle came through the line. "Come on, Cass. *Everybody* loves me."

"That's 'cause on the inside you're just a big ol' marshmallow." She grabbed a pair of black jeans and a freshly starched white shirt from her closet and laid them on the bed.

"Don't go spreading that around. You'll ruin my gambling reputation."

Cassie snorted. "Are you kidding? Your poker face is so good, no one would ever guess."

"If it was, I'd be playing in Vegas." Lonnie paused, then asked, "So, you coming in today?"

"Of course. The wicked don't rest on Sunday. Neither do I." She stretched her arms above her head. "Want breakfast from the diner?"

"I could go for a Daybreak Double."

"See you soon."

Cassie went into the bathroom. Waiting for the water to warm up, she leaned both hands on the counter and stared at herself in the mirror. She looked like she felt, which wasn't great. She'd thrashed about all night, tangling in sheets and punching her pillow as the previous evening with Bishop replayed on an endless loop.

As difficult as it was, she'd set aside the whole ethics thing as Marge had suggested and focused on what else he brought to the table. By the time they'd finished dinner, Cassie could no longer deny her attraction to him. *I mean, come on.* Not one person he'd crossed paths with had been able to resist those bulging biceps or his alluring smile. He was a good sport, and between his sense of humor and the smoldering looks he gave her...

Cassie turned off the warm water and splashed cold on her face, halfway expecting steam to rise from her skin. Her mind still spun with what-ifs. Maybe she should have considered a possible connection between Ashley and the trafficking case.

No. She slapped her cheeks, trying to wake herself up and disrupt the unhelpful second-guessing. Her investigation had been a continuation of her dad's, following the rules of law and logic. As he often said, hoofbeats most likely mean horses, not zebras.

Brushing her teeth, she thought back to Bishop's angry outburst at Palmer's house. That, along with his comments about anger management classes and the way he'd stormed out last night, belied his normal, sunny temperament. *What demons haunt you, Mr. Bishop?*

She pulled on her clothes, ran a brush through her hair and tugged it into the ponytail she always wore for work. Pinned on her badge, strapped on her gun, and she was out the door.

Her breakfast order sat ready on the front counter when she ran in. Marge would add it to her tab, so she grabbed the bag and made it back through the door before it swung shut. Not only was she late, she hadn't even started her incident report for the Palmer case. The Rangers would just love that.

She slowed as she passed Helen's desk, pulling a fresh prune Danish from the bag and handing it off to her like a relay baton.

Closing her office door behind her, Cassie slid into her chair and dialed Lonnie. "I've got the food."

"I'll bring coffee."

"Bring Helen a fresh cup, too. I got her one of those nasty prune pastries."

"She loves those things."

"I know. But you better promise me, if I ever reach the point where I crave a prune Danish, you'll do everyone a favor and put me down." She hung up on his laughter.

A few minutes later, Lonnie walked in carrying two steaming mugs. Sitting in one of the visitor chairs, he unwrapped the breakfast sandwich Cassie handed him.

"Bless Marge's little heart." He bit into a jalapeño bun stuffed with sausage, fried egg, melted cheddar, more jalapeños, bacon and hash browns.

"How can you even get that in your mouth?" Cassie unwrapped hers, which was half the size of Lonnie's.

"Just one of my many talents." Lonnie spoke around a mouthful of food. "What were you up to yesterday?"

Cassie took a bite of her sandwich and set it down. "Working on Dad's case. I came in early so the Rangers wouldn't bother me." She took a sip of coffee. "But not early enough."

He swallowed and wiped egg yolk from his mouth. "I can't believe they just ripped our case out from under us. It's ridiculous."

"I know. That's why I'm avoiding them. I don't want them pulling Dad's files away from me, too." Cassie lifted the top bun, picked off a piece of bacon and popped it in her mouth. "I know we're off the case, but *technically* the stash house hasn't been linked to the traffickers. So Sean's still trying to find the truck those neighbors saw there. And I've got Noah and Dave showing Jane Doe's picture around town again, trying to ID her."

Lonnie's laugh turned to coughing as he almost choked. "You've got those two working together? Let's have a meeting when they come back. I could use the entertainment."

"I've had enough of the back-and-forth sniping in our meetings. How much do *you* know about Dave?" Cassie trusted her cousin's input. He'd become a deputy a few years before she had, after her dad had tired of Lonnie's endless string of dead-end jobs and convinced him to take the exam and join the department. It had turned out to be the perfect fit for him.

"No more than anyone else. I think he's got an inferiority complex." Lonnie shrugged. "He's one of those guys who tries to build himself up by knocking others down. Off the clock, he runs with a rough crowd. I saw him one night at the Dead End, playing pool with a couple bikers. A skanky woman was hanging all over him. He finally passed her something from his pocket and she hightailed it to the restroom."

"Drugs?" Cassie would fire Dave on the spot if he was using. "Why didn't you report it to me?"

"I don't know what it was for sure. And she didn't come back out before I finished my beer and left." Lonnie set his sandwich down. "Probably wouldn't hurt to keep an eye on him."

Cassie drummed her fingers on her desk. "I'm glad you mentioned that. I have some concerns about Dave. From the first time I read his incident report on Dad's murder, I've thought he failed to follow protocol when he heard the shots. I think he froze in the backyard instead of immediately backing up Dad." At the time, she'd thought he'd panicked, and embarrassing him with a confrontation wouldn't have gotten her closer to the truth about her father's killers, so she'd let it go.

"Adam's mentioned that when they go out together, Dave hangs back, almost like he's scared."

"I think it would benefit him to be partnered with a more experienced deputy. Someone able to teach him procedures, judge his decisions."

"You thinking Adam?" He picked up his sandwich, leaning over the paper to take a bite.

"Nope."

Lonnie's mouth stalled in the open position and his gaze rose to meet Cassie's. "No. No, no, no." He dropped the sandwich back on the desk. "The last thing I need is some nitwit tagging along at my heels. Next thing you know, he'll accidentally shoot me. Or himself."

"Sorry." She gave her cousin an overly sweet smile. "You're the most qualified."

Giving Cassie the stink eye, he ripped off a chunk of sandwich with his teeth and chewed.

Cassie leaned back in her chair. "So, about the family dinner the other night."

Lonnie raised his brows.

"It concerned you, too. Thought I could fill you in on everything now."

"Sounds serious."

"The Rangers are actually here because they suspect someone within our department of being the leak." Cassie kept her voice low.

"Who told them we have a leak?" He picked up his mug.

Cassie shrugged. "But the concerning thing is, the only personnel records they requested are yours, mine, Adam's, Noah's and Dad's."

Lonnie swallowed a mouthful of coffee and began coughing. He set down his mug and got up, walking around Cassie's office. By the time he caught his breath, tears were running down his face.

Cassie handed him a tissue. "*That* went down the wrong pipe."

"No kidding." Lonnie dropped back into his chair. "How'd you find out about the personnel files?"

"It doesn't matter. What's important is that we know, so we can be wary of the Rangers. Just remember, you can't discuss this with anyone."

"I won't. But I appreciate you telling me." He wrapped up the rest of his sandwich and tossed it in the trash.

"Why, Lonnie Dixon. I've never seen you throw food away before." Cassie loved to rib her cousin about how much he ate and his expanding girth.

His brow furrowed. "Guess knowing the Rangers are looking at us took away my appetite."

"It may mean nothing." Feeling guilty for making him waste a sacred Daybreak Double, she tried to appease him. "But you know what they say, knowledge is power."

"You got that right." Lonnie stroked his beard, then seemed to shake it off. "Heard your PI friend put on quite a show at the Chute last night."

"News travels fast in these parts." Cassie grimaced, wondering whether her cousin had heard about Bishop riding the bull or making a scene.

Lonnie's brows arched. "Something going on between you two?"

Cassie's face warmed and she cursed her fair

complexion for always giving her away. "Lonnie, the guy just got into town a couple days ago."

"I can think of a few times that hasn't stopped you."

She balled up her sandwich wrapper and threw it at him. "Geez. Between you and Helen…"

"Why? What did Helen say?"

"She thinks he's my type, especially since he'll be leaving town soon."

"Well, you do seem inclined toward less commitment-heavy relationships." He gave her a knowing look.

Cassie huffed. "I don't see *you* settling down with anyone."

"Touché. Maybe it just runs in the family."

Cassie's smile faded. Lonnie was her cousin on her mom's side. His offhand remark meant no harm, but it was a reminder that her mother hadn't been made for a long-term relationship, either. One more thing Cassie had inherited from her.

"I better get back to work." Lonnie rose. "Thanks for breakfast."

Cassie gave him a thumbs-up. "Next time, you're buying."

Twenty minutes later, Helen knocked and opened Cassie's door without waiting for an answer. "Michael Pugh just called. He said he needs to talk to you, but he won't come in. He'll only meet you at that abandoned rest stop south of town, and he said to come alone."

Cassie arched a brow.

"He said it's about Ashley Bishop."

Chapter Thirteen

Obsessed with keeping an eye on Garrett Pugh, Bishop had just cruised past his house when Cassie called. Using her country directions, *Turn right at Jody's Gas-up, about three miles down take a left at the lightning-struck live oak, then a right where the street dead-ends*, he beat her to the abandoned rest stop. Only one car sat in the weed-filled parking lot. A beat-up, vintage green Impala matching the description of Michael's.

Cassie had told him to wait for her if he arrived first.

Not today, Sheriff. If this kid knew anything about Ashley's whereabouts, Bishop would make him talk, whether Cassie approved of his methods or not.

He parked near the car, able to see a silhouette in the driver seat. He climbed out of his truck and rounded the front of the Impala. Michael stared at him through the windshield. As Bishop reached the driver's-side door, it swung open full force, slamming him to the ground, knocking the breath out of him. The door handle hit him where nothing should *ever* hit a man. Waves of pain radiated to his groin, his stomach, finally settling deep in his core.

He'd grabbed on to the edge of the door as he fell, pulling it from Michael's grasp. Now he breathed through his pain and held on, hoping the kid didn't think to turn the key and back up. Before Bishop could stand, Michael leaped over him and started running.

Bishop staggered to the hood of the Impala, lifted it and pulled a spark plug. *That should slow you down, you little jerk.*

Moving easier now, he started after Michael. Bishop was fast, but so was the kid, and he had a good head start. Michael hurdled a crumbling knee-high brick wall and disappeared behind the locked restrooms. By the time Bishop rounded the building, the kid was hightailing it back to his car.

Gotcha. Despite the fury building within him, Bishop slowed his steps, reserving his energy in case the chase renewed. Michael, unable to start his car, was under the hood now. Skittish, he kept glancing over his shoulder as Bishop got closer. The kid was a mechanic, so finding the problem didn't take long. His lanky frame tensed, and he bolted again.

This time, the parking lot's loose gravel tripped the kid, and he went down hard. Probably took off a layer of skin. Served him right. But he was young, wiry, and he hopped up, taking off for an open grassy patch near a concrete table. The fall had done its trick, though, slowing him enough that Bishop was able to leap and tackle him.

The kid didn't surrender easily. He twisted and thrashed, his arms swinging and legs kicking like half an octopus. Bishop flipped him on his stomach, yanked his arms behind his back and cuffed him with one of the zip ties he always carried. The kid kept squirming, kept trying to kick Bishop.

"You want me to tether your ankles together, too, you little punk?"

The kid stilled.

"That's better. Now, where's Ashley?"

"What do you mean, where's Ashley? I thought you had her."

Not what Bishop expected to hear. He flipped the kid over, grabbed his shirt front, and yanked him to a sitting position. Bishop stepped back out of kicking range, glowering down on Ashley's supposed boyfriend. "Explain yourself."

Michael's angry stare changed to one of total confusion. "So, you really don't have her? Who *are* you?"

"I'm a private investigator, Michael. And I need answers from you."

The kid's eyes widened. "How do you know my name?"

"I'm a *good* private investigator. Now, where's Ashley?" The words came out as rough as the parking lot gravel. "She followed you to Resolute, right?"

"Yeah, but I didn't even know until she showed up at my door."

"Then you and she disappeared, along with both of your cars." Bishop took a step toward him. "The way I heard it, y'all ran off to get married." His hands, hanging by his sides, curled into now-familiar fists. "I want to know that she's okay, and where she is. *Now*." He barely registered his fists rising until Michael scooted back on his butt, cowering.

"Who told you that? Garrett?" The fear in Michael's voice disappeared, replaced by a cold, hard tone. "It's *his* fault that Ashley's gone. *I've* been looking for her for the last two days."

"What do you mean, it's Garrett's fault?" Bishop managed to lower his fist, though it was still clenched and ready. "And how would you know where to even start looking?"

"Garrett told me she might be between Resolute and El Campo somewhere off Highway 59. But after two days I realized I'd never find her just driving around. I needed Sheriff Reed's help." He sat taller. "I mean, I take full responsibility for everything. If she wasn't dating me, she never would have come here. And if I hadn't let her into that house, hadn't let her get near Garrett—"

"What did Garrett do?" Bishop spit the words one at a time, barely opening his mouth to let them out.

Michael stared at Bishop with haunted eyes. "He took her. My own brother…he took her." His face had gone from red to a pasty white, rivulets of sweat running down it. "He was always bad news, but I never thought he would ever do something this evil."

The fury in Bishop raged, and he didn't care who the target was. But as Michael spoke, his face wavered and the image of another kid, a girl about his age, superimposed itself there. His dead CI from Houston, taunting him. *What are you gonna do? Kill him, like you got me killed?* Bishop closed his eyes and shook his head. When he opened them, Michael stared at him with naked fear.

"Son of a sea biscuit! What do you think you're doing?" Cassie strode past Bishop and pulled Michael to his feet. Bishop hadn't even heard the crunch of her tires in the parking lot.

She pulled her tactical knife off her belt and tossed it to Bishop. "Cut that zip tie off of him *now.*"

Bishop glared at her. "I thought we agreed that you wouldn't interfere in the way I handle—"

She stepped up to him, toe-to-toe, her face inches from his. "And I told you to wait until I got here. Now cut that boy loose."

Still glaring, he flicked the knife open and slit the tie, letting it fall to the ground.

"Pick that up," she snapped at him. "We don't allow littering around here."

Bishop blew out an exasperated breath as he bent over for the tie. Afraid she'd make him pick up the rest of the trash, too, he didn't point out the plastic party cups and broken glass bottles near the building.

"I'm so sorry, Michael. Did he hurt you?" Cassie walked the kid toward the covered concrete table.

"Not really, Sheriff. Just scared me half to death. Thought he was one of the men who have Ashley."

Cassie froze midstep. "What men?"

"We were just getting to that." Bishop passed them and sat in the shade.

Michael sat on the far side of the table, shrinking in on himself like a balloon losing its air.

"Let's start at the beginning." Cassie settled near Bishop where she could look directly at the kid.

Michael scrubbed at his face with both hands. "I got news there was family trouble and rushed home to Resolute."

"When exactly was this?" Bishop asked. "And what was the family trouble?"

Michael jumped at his tone, but when Cassie nodded encouragingly, he began to talk. "Last weekend. Garrett called, said he'd gotten himself mixed up with some guys he shouldn't have. They were threatening to kill him."

Cassie rested her arms on the table. "What guys?"

"He didn't say then. Just said he needed me, so I raced back to Resolute to help him." Michael cringed at Bishop's disgusted expression. "What was I supposed to do? He's my brother. Me, him and Billy are all we have since Mom died."

"And the trouble?" Cassie prodded.

"Turns out he'd gotten involved with some gang that pimps out girls or something."

A lump formed in Bishop's stomach.

"But that wasn't even the worst of it." Michael averted his eyes. "He, uh, you see, those guys were mad because, well, because he lost one of the girls."

Bishop rose and leaned toward Michael, planting his fisted hands on the table. "Half-truths aren't gonna cut it, kid. What does 'lost' *really* mean?"

"He killed her, all right?" Michael blurted out. "Garrett was watching over some girls they had at some house, and he accidentally killed one."

Through clenched teeth, Bishop asked, "How did he *accidentally* kill a girl?"

"He said his job was to keep them doped up, but one of them either got too much or had a bad reaction to it. Whatever it was, she OD'd."

"Jane Doe." Cassie put her hand on Bishop's arm, pulling him back down next to her on the bench. "What does this have to do with Ashley?"

Michael's voice shook. "Those guys told Garrett if he didn't replace the girl immediately, they'd kill *him*."

Bishop's chest hurt like a mallet blow to his solar plexus. "So Garrett took Ashley as the replacement?"

"I beat the living daylights out of him, but it was already too late. Only thing that made me stop punching him was when he said they move girls along 59 toward Houston."

Suspicion snaked through Bishop's mind. "Wait a minute. If you beat your brother up, why didn't you stop him from taking Ashley in the first place?"

The kid's eyes filled with tears. "Because I wasn't there. I was mad at her for coming, 'cause her parents already hate me. We had a big fight, and I needed to get out of there, clear my head." He raked his hands through his hair and looked at them, pleading. "You gotta believe me. I *never* would have left her there if I knew what Garrett was going to do. I mean, he's my brother. I knew he was into some bad stuff, but kidnapping my girlfriend? I just didn't see it." Michael stared at him like a hungry man starving for absolution.

Bishop's anger and his fear for Ashley's safety had turned his heart to stone. He had no sympathy for Michael. Instead, he turned the knife again. "So you knew he was into some bad stuff, but you still left your little brother in Garrett's tender care."

"Ah, man, come on. I was seventeen when I left Resolute. I didn't have a job. I didn't have a place to stay. How was I supposed to take care of an eleven-year-old kid? I had to make a life in Houston before I could even think about bringing him there."

"Why didn't you call the sheriff right away, have her arrest Garrett and help find Ashley?"

"I could have helped, Michael," Cassie said.

"I thought about it. But Garrett said those guys could get to him even in jail. He'd be dead within a week." Michael hung his head. "And if we said anything to the cops about those guys, we'd all wind up dead. Even Ashley and Billy."

"Did he say they were local pimps?" Cassie's right hand was clenched on her thigh.

Michael shook his head. "No. He said they were part of a bigger group who had connections."

The lump in Bishop's stomach moved to his chest, squeezing the air from his lungs.

"Michael." Cassie waited until he met her eyes. "These guys aren't just pimps. They're human traffickers. They lure girls and young women, usually runaways or drug addicts, into a false sense of security. Pretend they care about them. Or get them hooked on drugs. Sometimes they just kidnap them."

Michael swallowed, looking like he was about to puke.

"They're like the wholesaler, selling to retailers. They move the girls along a circuit, sometimes working the girls themselves, but usually distributing them to pimps." Cassie's voice remained void of an incriminating tone, but its cold, detached tone made the words that much harder to hear. "The women are kept in cheap motels or massage parlors, or forced to work truck stops."

The color drained from Michael's face again.

Irrational or not, Bishop still partially blamed him for Ashley's situation. But that didn't mean he wanted Michael to get hurt. "Listen, kid. Don't go back to your house. You need to stay away from Garrett."

"What about Billy?"

"The sheriff and I'll pick him up. He can stay with you."

"I'll find somewhere safe for you to stay," Cassie said. "But you need to do as we say. I can't be chasing bad guys and worrying about you and Billy at the same time. Deal?"

The kid nodded, clearly defeated. "Just promise me you'll find Ashley."

Michael might not have been able to pound the truth out of his brother, but Bishop knew a lot of ways to make a man talk. And he'd use every last one of them on Garrett if he had to. Bishop stood. "Don't worry. That's a promise I intend to keep."

When they reached the parking lot, Cassie said, "Go directly to the justice center, Michael. I'll call Helen, let her know you're coming. Stay there until I make arrangements for you and Billy."

"Okay."

Bishop reached into his pocket. "You'll probably need this." He handed him the spark plug he'd removed earlier.

Michael started for his car, then stopped and turned back. "Hey, man, who *are* you?"

"The name's Bishop."

"Bishop?"

"I'm Ashley's uncle."

Michael closed his eyes. "She told me about you."

"Kid, whatever she told you, the truth is a hundred times worse."

After Michael drove off, Bishop braced himself for another scolding from Cassie.

"You did good, especially considering what we just learned." She scrutinized his face. "Are you okay?"

"Of course not. But at least—"

Cassie's phone rang and she held up a finger. "Sheriff Reed."

The voice coming through the phone was deep, muffled, and loud enough that Bishop could hear every word.

"If you want to know who killed your father, meet me at 1620 Oak Street in ten minutes."

The line went dead.

Chapter Fourteen

Bishop took a step toward her, his brows drawn together, but Cassie didn't have time to talk. She noted the time, then called her office.

"Sheriff's Department," Helen's brisk voice answered. "How may I—"

"It's me. Who's in the office?"

"Everyone's out right now. What's wrong?"

Cassie ran her palm across her hair. "Anyone in the vicinity of the old rest stop?"

"Hang on." Computer keys clicked. "Sean's the closest. About ten minutes away."

She checked the time again. Eight minutes left. "Never mind. Gotta go."

Cassie pocketed her phone and walked a short distance away. Her caller ID had said only Private Number. No name. *Has to be a setup.* She walked back. *But what if it isn't?* She stopped, the dust from her pacing settling on her boots.

She had to go. She had to check it out. She had to take backup. Cassie eyed Bishop, who looked concerned. Frustrated, but concerned. "You're coming with me."

As Cassie turned onto Oak Street, Bishop asked, "Think it's legit?" His tone expressed the same doubt plaguing Cassie.

"No way to know until we get there." She glanced at her watch again. Five minutes left. "But it sounds exactly like what happened to Dad. Best if we expect an ambush."

The address was part of a small residential neighborhood not far from the rest stop. Cassie parked two houses away, the only sound the tick of her engine cooling. No kids playing outside. No dogs barking. No neighbors talking or laughing.

Bishop surveyed the area. "It's too quiet."

"Yep." Cassie's head was on a constant swivel. "No splitting up."

They climbed out of the SUV and eased the doors closed. With guns drawn, they circled the house together, covering each other as they checked windows for signs of life. Nothing.

Returning to the front yard, Cassie observed the street. No curtains fluttered, dropped by the hands of neighbors peeking out to watch the excitement.

"You ever see that movie *Tombstone*?" Bishop whispered.

"When all the townsfolk skedaddled before the bullets started flying?"

They exchanged a knowing glance before climbing the porch steps and positioning themselves on either side of the door. She was glad he'd told her he used to be a cop. Without that experience, he might not know how to handle a situation like this. Turned out, Bishop made a pretty good partner.

He signaled her that he would kick it in. Cassie shook her head and pointed to herself. She was lead on this, and she aimed to follow protocol. Motioning for her to freeze, he cocked his head as if he heard something inside. Cassie paused, straining to pick up the sound. Then Bishop gave her a quick wink and stepped back, ready to assault the door.

Before he could, Cassie pounded on the door and yelled, "Sheriff Cassie Reed!"

As "Reed" came out of her mouth, Bishop's boot hit the door. It splintered from the frame and swung in.

Cassie dropped into a crouch where she'd been standing. "I told you to wait," she whispered.

Bishop's whisper matched her harsh tone. "You took away any advantage we had." He crouched on the opposite side of the doorway.

They held for a few seconds, then Cassie raised a brow toward Bishop. He nodded. Bishop went left, Cassie went right. They cleared the house, room by room, then moved on to the garage. Although the house had been completely empty, stacks of boxes filled the garage. While Bishop opened one to check its contents, Cassie stepped outside. She called Helen and asked her to run a search for the owner.

She rejoined Bishop, who had opened several more cartons. "What's in them?"

"Financial records." He moved to another stack and opened the top box. "But it looks like records for a bunch of different people."

"Maybe whoever owned this place was an accountant." As Cassie glanced around at the dusty garage, frustration fought with relief. She'd come here wanting answers, but at least she and Bishop were still alive.

Holding a ream of paper in one arm, Bishop flipped through it. "Maybe." He didn't seem in a hurry to leave.

"While you're doing this, I'm going back in the house." She needed to find at least a hint of who had lured her here.

She went in through the kitchen and opened drawers and cabinet doors. Not even a stray slip of paper in any of them. She turned down the short hallway that led to a small bedroom. A soft scraping noise stopped her. Rat? Possum? Critters always seemed to know when a house was vacant. Tipping her head, she strained to hear it again. Silence.

She stepped into the bathroom doorway next to her. She'd already cleared the room, finding nothing but a rusty water stain in the tub. A thump behind her made her spin, her peripheral vision catching movement in the mirror. The hallway ceiling revealed a square black hole. The wooden panel had been removed from the attic hatch. She swung her gaze to the access panel in the wall next to her, but before she could open it, a dark blur lunged from the bedroom and hit her full force.

He tackled her into the bathroom. She went down hard, her head slamming against the toilet. She kicked and flailed beneath him, trying to gain traction. When the figure, completely disguised in black, grabbed her shoulder, Cassie tightened her abs into a sit-up and rammed her forehead against his.

Stunned, he lost his grip on her. She jumped to her feet and tried to get past him, but he grabbed her by the ankles. When he yanked her feet out from under her, Cassie's chest hit the floor with a loud crack. *Son of a sea biscuit. That was a rib.* Searing pain spread through her torso. She broke his hold on one ankle and kicked back, connecting with his face. A satisfying crunch of nose cartilage fueled her fight, and she kicked again. He cried out and let go of her other ankle.

She made it into the hall and spun back toward the bathroom, pulling her gun. The perp still lay on his stomach, his mask dripping blood. He had beaten Cassie to the draw, a 9-millimeter in his outstretched hands.

She flung herself out of the doorway as a bullet just missed splitting her ponytail into pigtails. Cassie ran for the front door, pressing her radio mic and calling Bishop's name. As she reached the front porch, Bishop had already rounded the side of the house. A shot rang out and Cassie dropped, rolling behind a low brick wall lined with a hedge. Bishop took cover behind an oak tree and fired at the front door. Gun in hand, Cassie peeked over the hedge. After a moment of silence, a barrage of bullets flew from inside the house, and she and Bishop dropped flat. When the shooting stopped, Bishop raced to Cassie.

"Go! Don't let him get away." Bishop hesitated and Cassie got to her feet. "I'm fine. Get him."

Bishop ran toward the front door. Cassie followed him exactly two steps before losing her balance and falling. She fought to stand again, but the world spun, and vertigo took her to the ground.

"Cassie!" Bishop raced back to her side. "You *aren't* fine."

"Probably a minor concussion." She forced her eyes open. Bishop's face, lined with concern, hovered over her. "It was nothing. Just a collision with a toilet."

Bishop helped Cassie up. "You're bleeding." He held her arms out to the sides. "You've been shot."

"Can't be. I'm wearing a vest." *Just like Dad.* She watched blood soak her sleeve, cover her hand and drip off her fingers. "Well, if that don't snap my garters. I'm too busy to get..." Her vision blurred. "I think I need..."

Bishop eased her to the ground and called 911,

cradling her head in his lap. His fingers brushed across her forehead, soothing her.

She wasn't ready to meet her maker yet. But between the deep hum of Bishop's smooth voice as he talked to the dispatcher and the soft touch of his fingertips at her temples, Cassie was just fine with being babied a bit longer.

MINUTES LATER, or maybe hours, Cassie regained consciousness to the sound of sirens.

Another blink or two later, deputies and medics swarmed the scene.

One more and she found herself on a gurney.

"It's a flesh wound, Sheriff." A medic hooked her up to a bag of fluids. "A through-and-through on the underside of your arm." Cassie struggled to remain awake and professional while Noah and Adam paced around her, talking to Bishop.

And then Ranger Ward showed up. *A concussion, cracked ribs and getting shot wasn't enough for one day?*

Ward approached and crouched next to her. "You doing okay, Sheriff?"

Cassie gave him a thumbs-up. "Peachy keen 'n' hunky-dory."

The Ranger's mouth twitched at the corners.

"Why, Ranger Ward, I believe you're smiling. Didn't think you *could* smile."

"And I believe they've given you something for the pain."

Frowning, she looked at the medic, then at the bag of fluids he held above her. "Did you give me drugs?" she stage-whispered. "I'm on duty. I can't even have a drink when I'm on duty."

"We'll discuss this incident, and the call that brought you out here, tomorrow morning. My office." Ward stood.

"I'll be there bright and early." Dopey from the drugs, Cassie fought through them, unwilling to give any ground to the Ranger. "But we'll meet in *my* office." She gave him a satisfied grin. "And don't be late."

Ward started to reply, but his gaze traveled past Cassie, and his usual sour expression returned. "We'll also discuss why *he* shows up at all your crime scenes."

Cassie twisted her head as best she could to follow his line of sight. "Oh yeah, him." Bishop stood with arms crossed, a look of disdain aimed at the Ranger. "Don't worry about him. He's just my date."

She smiled at the look of amusement on Bishop's face before she blinked once more and was out.

Chapter Fifteen

That evening Bishop pounded on Cassie's front door, every swing of his fist carrying fear, frustration and anger.

Just hours ago he'd held her in his arms, silently begging whoever was in charge of such things to allow her to live. With her eyes closed and face in repose, the fierce, tenacious sheriff had faded to a fragile shadow of herself.

But apparently, the old Cassie had returned somewhere between the ambulance driving off and the obstinate sheriff checking herself out of the hospital against medical advice.

"Cassie! Open the door." He kept pounding.

"Excuse me." The soft voice behind Bishop stopped him mid-pound. "Are you looking for Cassie?"

He turned around to find a middle-aged woman wearing cropped jeans, an oversize blue shirt with the sleeves rolled up, and camo-green Crocs.

"I'm her neighbor." She waved in the direction of the house next door. "I couldn't help but hear you."

"Sorry." Bishop grimaced. "Didn't mean to disturb you." He took a deep breath, trying to calm down. "I'm a friend of Cassie's. Did you happen to see her come home earlier?"

Every neighborhood had at least one nosy buttinsky, eager to share the fruits of their meddling. Bishop hoped Camo Crocs was Cassie's.

"No, I've been working in the garden all day." She tipped her head to the side and tapped a finger against her lips, as if trying to decide if he meant Cassie harm. His disappointment must have looked convincing, because she took pity on him. "But if she's not answering the door, there's a good chance she's out back in her studio."

"Studio?" Bishop came off the porch to continue the conversation.

The neighbor nodded. "Well, she calls it a shed, and she doesn't know I know about it. So mum's the word."

Bishop gave her a polite smile. "Thank you, ma'am. I'll go 'round back, see if she's there."

"There's a gate over here." She led him to the side of the house nearest hers. "I only know about her studio because sometimes I sneak into Cassie's yard and water her plants for her. She's a wonderful girl, but she kills plants like nobody's business."

"Except yours," Bishop mumbled under his breath.

They reached the gate, and Bishop managed to make it through while leaving Ms. Buttinsky on the other side. He rounded the back corner of Cassie's bungalow and paused. Not sure what he'd expected, but this was definitely not it.

A path of slate stepping-stones crossed the center of the lawn, beginning at the patio and ending in front of the shed's door. Flowering bushes lined the fences surrounding the yard, and arching trellises strained beneath the weight of several bougainvillea. Bishop glanced at the patio's single cushioned chair, positioned beside a small table. A book and one coaster sat on the table's mosaic top.

He stayed on the stone pathway to the shed, conflicting emotions still battling within him. And now another, curiosity. A large padlock hung from a metal hasp near the door handle. Bishop tried the handle, finding it locked, too. After no response to his knock, he walked around the small building. No back door. A few windows, one blocked by a window unit AC. The others were covered by curtains. He returned to the front of the shed.

"Just what do you think you're doing?" Cassie's angry voice carried across the yard from the patio. "Get away from there."

She moved from stone to stone, wincing as she charged him in slow motion. Her wet hair hung loose, water drops soaking the straps of her light blue tank top. White shorts ended mid-thigh, and as each shapely leg stretched to the next piece of slate, five sparkling purple toenails twinkled at Bishop. *Glitter?*

He pushed his curiosity aside, his concern and frustration taking center stage. "What are *you* doing here? You're supposed to be in the hospital."

"Says who? You?" Glowering at him, Cassie reached the end of the path.

"Yeah, me. And your doctor. You checked out AMA."

"I swear, I'm gonna arrest you if you keep digging into people's private business. How'd you find out I left against medical advice?"

"Noah told me the last time I tried to see you."

"That boy. I'm gonna—wait." The anger in her voice drained away, replaced by confusion. "What do you mean *last* time? You never came to the hospital."

"Are you kidding? I showed up so many times, the receptionist got sick of my face. You were either with the doctor, in X-ray or some other excuse. They wouldn't even tell me what floor you were on." Bishop threw his hands up in a very un-anger-management fit of pique. "It wasn't until I talked to Noah that I found out the real reason."

"And what was that?" Cassie folded her arms, then flinched in pain and dropped them to her sides. But not before drawing Bishop's attention to her chest. He had to blink before he could force his eyes to meet hers.

"They were afraid your attacker would make another appearance." He managed to bring his thoughts back on track. "Finish the job."

"That's ridiculous. A coward who hides behind a ski mask wouldn't take a chance like that." She shifted her stance, wincing again. "I need to sit down." She turned and followed the path back to the patio.

Bishop came right behind, admiring her long legs, revealed for the first time since he'd met her. "I'd offer to carry you, but if you have broken ribs—"

"I don't need to be carried," she snapped. Then more softly, "They're not broken. Just bruised." She lowered herself onto the chair, breathing shallow breaths. "Not sure bruised hurts any less than broken, though." She picked up a glass from the coaster. "You can grab a chair from the table inside. And there's iced tea in the fridge if you want some."

"Sweet?"

"Of course."

"Think I'll pass." Stepping into her kitchen, Bishop found it pretty much as he'd imagined. Spotless, organized, the countertops clear of small appliances except a coffee maker. He continued on to the table and picked up a chair, pausing to check out Cassie's living area. Again, not surprising. A couch, a coffee table with nothing on it, and a TV against the wall. Orderly, like the lady sheriff herself.

When he returned to the patio, Cassie eyed him as he placed the chair at the opposite side of the table. "You were gone long enough. Check out the whole place?"

"I would never dig into people's private business." He feigned a look of innocence as he tossed her words back at her.

"Yeah, right." She paused, then changed the subject. "I called Helen from the hospital. She said she found a place for Michael and Billy to stay." Cassie smiled. "Thanks for picking up Billy."

"No problem. Figured I'd run a few errands between trips to see you. I hoped to find Garrett there, too, take care of both things at the same time." He blew out a frustrated breath. "But he wasn't at the house."

"We can go tomorrow morning. I know you're worried about Ashley, but if Garrett wasn't there, he's probably in the wind."

"I can handle trying the house again. You should take it easy for a few days."

"I'm fine. Just a little sore."

Bishop raised a brow. "What else did the doctor say besides bruised ribs?"

"Minor concussion. And the bullet didn't hit anything important. Absolutely no reason to stay in the hospital."

"Maybe they were just trying to keep you safe."

"Like I said, whoever it was isn't going to waltz into a hospital for another go at it." She sighed, leaning her head back against her chair and closing her eyes for a moment. "Besides, I'm more comfortable at home. I don't like anyone hovering over me. Never have."

"I bet you loved it when you were a kid and your mom hovered."

A cloud crossed Cassie's face. "If she ever did, I can't remember it. But Mom wasn't the hovering type."

"She's gone?"

Cassie nodded.

"I'm sorry." The image of a young Cassie graveside hurt his heart. "How young were you when she died?"

"She didn't die." Cassie met his gaze and gave him a tight smile. "Just…disappeared. Ran off, I guess. I was eleven. We came home from school one day and she just wasn't there."

"No note? Nothing?"

Cassie shook her head. "I called my dad, and he came straight home. All I remember after that is him hugging me. Dad wasn't much of a hugger. Guess that's why I remember it so well. It was the only time he gave me a really tight, long hug." Her face flushed. "I felt so guilty about enjoying that hug."

"Why?"

Her gaze drifted to the live oak, as if lost in memory. "I thought that if Mom running off was what it took to finally get some attention from Dad, I was glad she was gone." Her sad eyes returned to Bishop. "But that wasn't true. I idolized her."

Bishop couldn't imagine growing up without being smothered by parental love.

"Dad was more of a man's man," Cassie said. "He never really knew what to do with a daughter, so he treated me like another son. At least, until Mom disappeared. Then all of a sudden I was in charge of my brothers, the housework, cooking, everything."

"How could you idolize your mom if she abandoned you?"

A wistful smile touched her lips. "Mom wasn't a creature of this world." She cocked a brow toward Bishop. "Maybe she was from your woo-woo world. She was like a hippie, a fairy, a free spirit who danced without touching the ground. I loved her." The condensation from her glass had pooled on the coaster, overflowing onto the mosaic tabletop. Cassie trailed a finger through it. "She was unapologetically her authentic self, and I wanted to be exactly like her."

After a moment of silence, she straightened her back and moaned in pain. "At least, I did until she left. Then I realized the full consequences of her actions on our family."

"What do you mean?"

"Mom refused to become the wife that Dad wanted." Cassie's voice was back to the no-nonsense quality Bishop was used to. "She put her artistic interests before the rest of us. Dad yelled and Mom refused to engage. She'd just go out to her studio." She flickered a quick glance at her shed. "I guess one day she got tired of the yelling."

Bishop paused for a moment, then took advantage of the obvious segue. "What's in your shed over there?"

Lifting one shoulder with nonchalance, Cassie said, "Nothing. Why?"

"Just curious. You seemed pretty upset that I was near it."

She tried straightening in her chair but stopped with a wince. "I didn't expect to find you in my backyard. That's all."

"Then show me your studio."

Cassie whipped her head toward him and narrowed her gaze. "Why'd you call it a studio?"

"Well…" Bishop leaned forward and lowered his voice. "I'm not supposed to tell you, but your neighbor happened to mention—"

"When were you talking to my neighbor?" The anger was returning.

"While I was pounding on your door and yelling your name," Bishop said, amused at how hostile she became over a shed.

She massaged her temples. "What else did the old snoop tell you?"

Bishop chuckled. "That's all. How 'bout you show me what you're hiding inside?" When she wouldn't reply, he tried a different approach. "Whatever you do in that shed is a part of you. And I want to know *everything* about you."

Cassie lowered her eyes. "What I do in there is personal."

"This is starting to sound a little kinky." He waggled his brows when she glared at him. "Seriously, why such a big secret? You know about all my woo-woo stuff."

Her lips twitched into a smile. The look she gave him was almost pleading, but what was she pleading for? To be left alone? Or did she really want to share her secret? Either way, it had to be her decision.

"You really want to know everything about me?" She rested her arm on the table. "Because you might not like what you find."

"Then that would be my problem, not yours." Bishop reached across the table and stroked the back of her hand. "And yes, Sheriff Cassie Reed, I really want to know everything."

Her smile was bittersweet as she rose. "Hang on a minute. I have to get the key."

She returned and he followed her to the shed, unable to even guess at what he was about to see. Cassie unlocked the padlock, pulled the door open and stepped in, pausing to flip a light switch. Bishop walked in behind her, his mouth dropping open.

HER HEART PUMMELING her sore ribs, Cassie watched him. The first person she'd allowed into her studio. The first person she'd revealed her whole self to.

Bishop didn't speak. He didn't move. He just stood still, taking it all in. She followed his gaze, trying to see the room through his eyes. Tarps covered the floor. Her pottery wheel stood in the middle of the room. Shelves on one wall held supplies, while another displayed finished pieces. Or rather, *un*finished pieces.

"Wow. Not what I was expecting." He stepped to the wheel and examined it more closely, then looked at Cassie. "Why is this something you hide?"

She dragged her teeth against her lower lip. "Because when I come out here, I turn into my mother. I get lost in it with no sense of time." She pointed to an old-fashioned two-bell alarm clock near the wheel. "I don't start throwing clay until I've set that alarm. When it goes off, I quit, no matter where I'm at. Otherwise, I'd forget about everything else I'm supposed to do, and that's not how responsible people act."

Bishop walked over to the shelves holding her art and picked up a piece. After examining it, he set it down with care.

"You don't have to be so careful with those. They're all horrible."

"They're not horrible." He picked up one of her favorites, a vase. She'd lost control of its mouth, but the wavy opening had turned out even better. "This one is incredible." He replaced it with the next in line. He looked at her, then back at the piece. "Some of them just look unfinished."

"That's because most of them are." She stored clay projects in plastic wrap, returning to them when time allowed. "Some I've lost interest in. I usually break them into pieces and toss them in my reclaimed clay bucket."

Bishop held up one that resembled an alien with a long snout.

Cassie laughed. "Some I've stopped and started so many times, I can't even remember what they were supposed to be."

Bishop set it back on the shelf and crossed to the wheel. "I don't know anything about pottery. Tell me how all this stuff works."

She assessed him, wondering if he was serious or just humoring her. When he continued to stare at her in earnest, she relented.

"You start with a fresh lump of clay and wedge all the air out." At his questioning look she said, "Squish, basically. Then you fasten it to the bat." She showed him the center of the wheel. "Moisten your hands, and center the clay."

"Make sure it's exactly in the middle of the table?"

"Yes, but there's more to it than that. You wrap your hands around it and cone up, then down, over and over." She showed him the motions with her hands. "As you're doing that, you listen to it. It'll tell you what it wants to become."

"The *clay* tells *you*?" Bishop's face looked like hers probably had when he talked about his meditation.

"That's what I've read. If it's true, I'm obviously not listening well." She scoffed at herself. "Once the clay spins beneath my fingers, I just zone out. All the stress and pressures of life just…disappear."

"Cassie, this is as much a part of you as shooting guns and arresting felons. You should stop hiding it."

It came from her mother, this desire for artistic creation. Cassie's soul cried out for it like an addict screaming for drugs, refusing to quiet until the craving was appeased. At the same time, her mind stalled in fear. Fear that if she allowed it to, the desire would swallow her whole, tear her away from everyone she loved.

"I don't want anyone else to know. Please don't make me regret letting you in." She hated the pleading tone in her voice.

The intensity of Bishop's gaze pulled at her heart. "It's not mine to tell." He crossed the short distance and wrapped his arms around her, careful not to squeeze her ribs. "But I hope one day *you'll* share it with the world. Or, you know, at least the rest of Resolute."

Thankful that the levity in his voice broke the tense moment, Cassie chuckled. "I'm not so sure Resolute is the best place for artistic appreciation."

"Maybe not," he said into her hair, still holding her to him. "But *I* appreciate it."

Slowly, he lowered his head to hers and paused, as if waiting for her to shove him away. But she didn't. She didn't have the energy to fight what she hadn't even realized she wanted. And what she wanted more than anything at this exact moment was Tyler Bishop's lips on hers.

She rocked forward, speeding up the process, and she could swear Bishop's lips curved into a smile before opening, his tongue sliding alongside hers.

Cassie sank into it, her fingers hooking into his belt loops, the only thing keeping her grounded. Bishop's hands loosened from around her, and he cradled her head in them, his thumbs brushing away tears she hadn't known she'd cried.

It was the most vulnerable she'd ever allowed herself to be in front of someone. No badge, no gun, surrounded by the evidence of her own whimsy. And yet with Bishop, she didn't feel scared or embarrassed. She felt free.

Bishop pulled back, concern warring with passion in his expression. "Are you okay?" He brushed away another tear. "Did I hurt you?"

Cassie brought her arms up, her right hand sliding behind his head. "I'm fine." She pulled him closer. "I've never felt better." She touched her lips to his once more, chasing the feeling of freedom.

They continued to touch, to explore, eventually making their way to her sparse, utilitarian bedroom. She glanced at Bishop's face as he took in the room. She'd never allowed a man in her home before, let alone her bedroom. Always in control, she preferred to scoot out of the man's place before sunrise, before things got awkward. But Bishop was different.

Standing by the bed, she followed his gaze around the room. "It's kind of simple."

Bishop stepped to her, stopping only inches away. Lifting her hair from her shoulders, he let it slide slowly through his fingers. "I like it."

He tipped her chin up with one finger and kissed her, a soft caress of her lips that had her hungering for something deeper, something more fervent. But Bishop kept it tender, brushing his lips against hers until the heat building within consumed her.

Cassie grabbed the front of Bishop's shirt, tugging him to the bed and pushing him to sit. She lifted her tank top, nearly staggering when her ribs screamed out in protest.

Bishop stood, his hands reaching out to steady her. "Are you okay? Maybe we shouldn't…" He trailed off as if reluctant to finish the thought.

His concern made her want him that much more.

"I'm made of sterner stuff than that." She turned around, pulling her hair to the side. "Can you manage a bra clasp?"

He scoffed, as if affronted by her lack of faith in him. "Oh, I can manage."

But instead of reaching right for it, Bishop trailed his fingers up and down her spine. The warmth of his hands settled above her waist before reaching around and undoing the top button of her shorts.

Cassie's short and fast breaths had nothing to do with her ribs.

The sound of the zipper seemed impossibly loud, as tooth by tooth it lowered and her shorts slipped from her body.

His lips replaced his hands, kissing her back, her neck, her shoulders while his hand settled itself lower.

There was nothing to worry over, nothing more to focus on than the fire building inside.

Cassie's head dropped back on a moan, and her legs weakened as her pleasure reached its peak, again and again.

When she finally stilled, Bishop unhooked her bra, kissing her newly exposed skin.

It took a few deep breaths, but finally Cassie's legs felt stable enough to move. Turning in his arms, she faced him. Let her bra fall to the floor between them.

His gaze roamed from the top of her auburn hair all the way to her sparkly purple toes and back up again. She was battered, bruised and pleasure-worn. She had never felt more beautiful.

Hooking her thumbs into her panties, she slid them to the floor.

Bishop licked his lips.

She grabbed the hem of his T-shirt and lifted.

She had to grit her teeth when her arms went past rib height.

Bishop saw. "Now, just hold on. I think maybe we've done enough for tonight. It's no fun if you're in pain."

Her want, her need, overruled her injuries. She unbuckled his belt, and in a matter of seconds the rest of his clothes were on the floor. Cassie ran her hands across the well-defined planes of his chest, gently touched the bruises covering his abs.

She smiled and pushed him back on the bed. "Oh, we're doing it, Mr. Bishop." She straddled him, loving the way his eyes centered on hers. "You're not the only one who can ride a bucking bull, you know."

At that, Bishop chuckled.

Then there was nothing but them, two bodies moving together, each healing the other in ways that had nothing to do with their external wounds.

He was gentle.

She wasn't.

It was perfect.

And as sleep finally overtook her, cradled in Bishop's arms, Cassie realized all her pain was gone.

Chapter Sixteen

Early the next morning, Bishop eased Cassie's front door shut so he wouldn't wake her. He smiled to himself. He'd come over bound and determined to stay, keep an eye on her. After all, she did have a concussion. But he hadn't planned on how close she'd let him get. How far they'd take their relationship. Most of the time, Cassie riled him up in both the best and worst of ways. But last night it was as if they'd become one, their chakras completely aligned.

He laughed to himself, imagining Cassie's expression if he told her that.

His mood darkened, though, as he parked in front of Garrett's house. Cassie's injuries had been only part of the reason he didn't want her here. He planned on getting the information about the traffickers from Garrett any way he could, and the sheriff might not like some of his methods. Though Garrett hadn't been at the house yesterday, Bishop wasn't convinced the kid had fled for good. He didn't figure him for being smart enough to do precise risk assessments.

After a night's rest—well, some of it was rest—Bishop was ready to take on the lying piece of crap who could lead him to his niece.

Bishop crossed the front porch and pounded on the flimsy door. He gave Garrett a minute before pounding harder, then tested the knob. When it turned in his hand, he pushed the door open.

Garrett, a few feet away from the door, froze, his eyes widening. "What the…" He came at Bishop with both arms stretched straight out, as if to push him back outside.

Instead, Bishop grabbed Garrett and pushed *him* up against the wall.

"What are you doing, man?"

"I'm getting the truth out of you one way or another. I already know you're working for the human traffickers and that you gave Ashley to them."

"I don't know what you're talking about." Garrett made a feeble attempt to bat at Bishop's arms. "Get off me."

"Who are they? Where did they take Ashley?" Bishop's right hand balled into a fist.

"How should I know, man? I just babysit their bit—"

He punched Garrett in the stomach. Hard. "Never call a woman that. Especially not my niece."

Garrett doubled over and slid down the wall. When he struggled to get up from the floor, Bishop grabbed the front of the kid's shirt and hauled him up. He shoved him against the wall again, one hand on his chest, the other around his throat. Tight enough to scare him. Loose enough that he could speak.

"I heard in addition to babysitting, you dope them up. Only this last time, you gave one of the girls too much. She died from an overdose, and you hid her body in the shed behind the stash house."

"Look, I don't know where you're getting your information—"

Bishop pulled back the hand from Garrett's throat and punched him in the face. This time the punk didn't even try to get up. Bishop hauled him to his feet again. Propped him against the wall again.

"I'm running out of patience. Either you tell me everything you know about the whole operation, or I'll dispose of you like you did that girl."

Blood and snot ran down Garrett's face. "Try it, and they'll find you. And you don't want to know how they get rid of people."

"Then maybe I'll just put out the word that you're cooperating with the police in the murder. And apprehension of the entire ring." Bishop leaned forward, close enough to see Garrett's eyes dilate in fear. "Keep my hands clean, let them do the dirty work for me."

"You don't even know who they are. You just said so." Garrett's voice lost some of its defiance.

Bishop shrugged, the nonchalant movement at odds with the tension in his chest. "I don't have to. I just have to spread the word. It'll get to them." He smiled and Garrett flinched. "I'll just watch you, and after they've disposed of you, I'll take care of them."

Sweat dripped down Garrett's temples. A few more minutes, maybe a few more punches, and Garrett would spill his guts. Bishop pulled his fist back for another jab.

"What do you think you're doing?" Cassie's voice came from right behind him.

Bishop's stomach dropped. Without turning around, he said, "I'm allowing Garrett to live in exchange for information about the trafficking ring."

Cassie shifted to his side. From the corner of his eye he saw her cross her arms, looking like a teacher about to go into full-on lecture mode. "You can't just beat it out of him."

Bishop hung his head, muttering a curse Cassie would not approve of. Why did she have to show up now?

"I told him that, Sheriff. I told him he can't kill me." Garrett's upper lip curled into a sneer aimed at Bishop. "You're gonna be sorry you ever messed with me."

"Shut up." Cassie stepped closer to the two men. "And don't think you'll be getting off any easier when I haul you down to the jail. We've got a couple of Texas Rangers in the house, and they're awfully interested in this whole gang you've hooked up with. I'm sure they'll want to question you, too."

She looked Garrett over from head to toe, pure disgust on her face. "And yeah, they may be more gentle than Mr. Bishop here, but don't be fooled. 'Cause when they haul you back to their Austin headquarters, where the really bad guys go, they'll throw you to the wolves. And how do you think a little small-town pup like yourself will fare, hmm?"

Garrett struggled against Bishop, who pushed him harder.

"Let him go, Bishop." Cassie's voice was firm. But it was the look of hurt in her eyes that finally made him act.

"Fine." He took his hands off the kid so fast, Garrett collapsed on the floor, gasping. Bishop turned to Cassie. "He was about to tell me everything."

"And you think that makes what you're doing okay? You can't beat a confession out of someone you're interrogating. Actually, you're not supposed to be interrogating him at all." Cassie blew out a breath of frustration. "That's why I wanted to come along today, instead of *taking it easy.*" She glared at him.

Bishop held his hands up in surrender. "Go ahead, do it your way. But you might want to cuff him so he can't—"

Pain exploded in Bishop's knee and he went

down, his flailing arms grabbing at Cassie, bringing her down, too.

"What—" Cassie moaned, holding her side as she tried to untangle herself from Bishop.

"Punk kicked me in the knee." The back door banged, and Bishop struggled to stand, then helped Cassie to her feet. She hobbled out the front door, one hand still on her ribs. After a few limping steps, Bishop picked up speed and followed Garrett out the back.

Bishop checked the garage first. Empty. The back of the property stretched all the way to a small creek. He ran as fast as his knee allowed, scouring the area. No sign that Garrett had come this way.

Limp-running back toward the house, he heard a car engine turn over. Bishop pushed himself harder. He hopped the short fence to the driveway, groaning when his knee buckled on the landing.

The Mustang was gone.

So was Cassie's SUV.

As he speed-hobbled to his truck, Bishop pulled out his phone. He had no idea which way Garrett had fled, but that wouldn't stop him from joining the hunt. He tapped Cassie's number, frustrated when he had to leave a message to call him with her location.

Before he could pull away from the curb, though, Cassie's SUV came down the street toward him and pulled into the driveway. Bishop shut off his truck and limped up the drive, eager for another go at Garrett.

But when she slammed her door and stomped across the yard alone, his anger toward Cassie returned. He followed her to the porch steps, where she stopped to brush at dirt and grass stains on her clothes.

"I couldn't catch up to him." Failure added a hard edge to her voice. "I checked his car first. He wasn't there, so I moved down the street, checking side yards and anywhere else he might be hidden. I must've been five houses down when I heard his car start. I tried to run back, but he was coming toward me when I was still a couple houses away." She looked into Bishop's eyes. "The dadgum son of a sea biscuit swerved up on the grass and tried to run me down. I got my car and went after him fast as I could, but I never even caught a glimpse of that Mustang."

Bishop was relieved she hadn't been hit. But right now, so much rage filled him from the little weasel slipping through his fingers that he couldn't fully register any other emotions. And Garrett's escape was all on Cassie.

He brushed past her without a word, stepped over the dog who never moved, and went back in the house. Cassie's footsteps followed him.

"Look, Bishop, don't think that just because I don't condone beating a confession out of someone, I don't care—"

"Save it, Sheriff. We both know you only care about doing things by the book. Now, if you'll excuse me, I have a house to search. *Illegally.*"

CASSIE BIT HER tongue until the metallic tang of blood hit her throat. It was that or cry, and she'd be darned if she'd shed tears over this aggravating Jekyll-and-Hyde act Bishop was playing.

Last night, when the world hadn't ended while she showed him her studio, she'd thought they had both turned a corner. That by showing him the part of her she didn't trust anyone else with, things would be different.

What a joke.

Before drifting off to sleep, they'd agreed to question Garrett together. But when she woke, Bishop was already gone. Her gut told her he hadn't gone out for coffee and bagels, and she was glad she listened to it. She should've listened to it last night when she'd seen him poking around her studio and just kicked him out.

Because when she found him at the Pugh house, trying to choke the truth out of Garrett, she broke a little inside. Not because Bishop was beating up someone lower than a snake's belly in a wheel rut. The punk had earned that whupping. No, she broke because she'd ignored her own rules. She'd let Bishop get too close.

What she had thought was freedom was really just unrealistic romantic notions, the kind her mother was known for.

"Make sure you wear gloves." That's all she would say about him searching the house. Cassie snapped on her own pair before stepping into a bedroom. It was no more legal for her to search the house than Bishop, but at least she had a reason to be here. She needed to pack a few more clothes for Billy.

Two unmade twin beds with a nightstand between them filled most of Billy's room. Clothes were strewn across the floor, but a few shirts hung in the tiny closet. Searching dresser drawers, Cassie managed to round up several T-shirts and a couple more pairs of jeans that still smelled of detergent and fresh air from hanging on a clothesline.

She found socks and underwear in the top dresser drawer, all in a jumbled pile. Cassie pulled out a week's worth of each and carried everything out to her SUV. She returned to the house and looked into another room. *Must be Michael's.* It was empty except for a neatly made bed and a dresser. She looked through the drawers, but they were as vacant as the closet.

Bishop had started in the kitchen but was already in the master bedroom by the time Cassie walked in. Garrett had obviously taken over the master after the boys' mother died, because it looked like an adult version of Billy's room. Unmade bed, dirty clothes everywhere, nudie magazines sprawled across the floor.

His hands gloved, Bishop searched the night-stand drawers. He glanced over at her, his expression neutral. Cassie matched it and walked to the dresser.

She found a 9-millimeter handgun hidden beneath an unfolded pile of T-shirts. She'd seen the shotgun leaning against the wall in a corner when she'd come in. A rush of heat burned through her like a flash fire. Had *Garrett* killed her father?

Cassie left them where they were. *For now.* She'd have to get a warrant, and she didn't have probable cause to request one at this point. She moved on to the closet. A few shirts on hangers, but most of them were on the floor covering his shoes. She reached up to the top shelf and felt along until her fingers grasped a bundle. She took it down, set it on the bed, and unwrapped it. Inside the dirty T-shirt she found a brick of heroin. She wrapped it back up, put it on the shelf, and continued searching.

By the time she finished, she'd come across at least a half pound of weed and a baggie of cocaine, in addition to the heroin. Were these the drugs he used to dope the girls? Or were they payment for his evil deeds?

Bishop, done with pulling everything from dirty plates to dust bunnies out from under the bed, stood and popped his back. "Not even a hint of where they're holding the girls."

"No, but enough drugs to put him away for a good while," she said, her voice as neutral as his expression. "And if the guns match to any crimes, even longer."

"But we're just leaving it all here, for him to come back and collect at his convenience." Bishop scoffed and walked out of the room.

Cassie went after him, catching up on the front porch. "You think I don't want to arrest his scrawny butt? But you know darn well it won't stick unless we do everything right."

He turned and gave her a look sharp with disappointment that cut deep into her heart. Then he stepped off the porch, walked to his truck and drove away.

For the first time in a long while, Cassie cursed. And just as she'd never admit out loud that Garrett deserved Bishop's punches, she'd never tell a soul how good it felt to let the profanity slip past her lips.

She'd closed the front door and was stepping over the dog when her phone rang.

"Perfect timing, Helen. I need you to put out a BOLO on Garrett Pugh's car."

"Where *are* you?" Helen whispered in a frenzied tone.

"Taking care of some things. Why?"

"You were supposed to be here early to meet with the Rangers." Helen's voice dropped even lower. "That one guy, Ward, he's fit to be tied."

"Dang it. I completely forgot about that." She scrubbed a hand down her face. "But to be fair, I was on drugs at the time. *And* had a concussion. Think that's a good enough excuse for him?"

"I think you better get yourself to the office PDQ." The call ended.

Chapter Seventeen

"Reed! In our office. Now."

Cassie had made it as far as her office door when Ward's voice bellowed down the hallway. He stood outside their room, his hands on his hips.

She turned to face him. "It's *Sheriff* Reed. You want to talk to me, you come to my office."

"Won't be for much longer." His voice was softer, but still plenty loud for Cassie to hear.

She rounded her desk and sat, composing herself. Boots drummed along the marble floor, the echo no doubt Mills's footsteps. They entered her office and Mills shut the door. Neither bothered to sit.

"Did you not understand me when I told you to stay away from the trafficking case?" Ward asked. He looked like a cartoon character with steam coming out of his ears.

"I understood perfectly. And I did what you, uh, *demanded*." It definitely hadn't been a request.

His left eye ticked. "Then explain that fiasco yesterday."

"If by fiasco, you mean me getting beat up and shot, what makes you think that had anything to do with the traffickers?" Cassie cocked a brow at Ward. "Or the leak, which is supposedly the only thing you're investigating."

"Just tell us what you were doing at that house." Mills was still playing the good cop, keeping his voice gentle and his face neutral. Too neutral.

Cassie stared hard at him for a moment, finally seeing through a crack in his mask. He was even more devious than Ward, who'd made it clear from the get-go what he thought of her.

"I don't owe you an explanation about any of our cases." Cassie stood. Enough of the psychological advantage of towering over your opponent. "Unless I request your assistance with a case, you have no jurisdiction here."

Ward crossed his arms. "We do when it's an internal affairs investigation."

"Then explain to me how yesterday's abandoned house has anything to do with *that* investigation."

"We have confidential information linking it to the traffickers," Mills said.

"And when did you receive this confidential information?" Cassie smoothed her hair. "Prior to yesterday? Or after I was shot?"

Mills stole a sidelong glance at Ward that answered her question.

"So someone around here is keeping tabs on what I do, where I go, then telling you it's somehow involved with the traffickers." She smirked. "How convenient for you. And your informant. Has it ever occurred to you that maybe your informant *is* the leak? Maybe you're the ones internal affairs should be looking at."

Another look from Mills to his partner. Ward ignored him this time.

"And what about the Palmer house? Somebody tell you that one's part of the leak, too?" Cassie's fingernails were halfway through her palm by now. "How about you give me a list of every address that's off-limits to my deputies and me. Right now. That way we'll know where to stay away from, and if the address isn't already on the list, you'll know your informant is feeding you a bag of grade A cow manure."

"That won't be necessary."

"Why is that?"

"Because we've already met with the county council, and as of immediately you are relieved of duty until we've completed a full investigation." Ward's smug smile made Cassie want to punch him in his Texas-sized nose.

But she wouldn't give them the satisfaction of seeing her emotions. "On what grounds?"

"You're impeding our case. Interfering in the search for justice regarding this internal leak. The council agreed to name a replacement for you."

Mills jumped in. "Depending on how things

fall out after we're through here, you may be re-instated."

Cassie reeled. If the council brought in some stranger who didn't know the county, didn't know the people of Resolute… "Who did they choose as my replacement?"

"Lonnie Dixon. He's chief deputy, which makes him the logical choice." Ward's tone turned even more condescending. "And our investigation to date shows he's not connected to the leak."

Cassie sighed with relief. She could trust Lonnie to run the department the way she and Dad had. But that single fact did nothing to allay her anger. A deeper understanding of Bishop's pain and frustration burrowed into her. He'd mentioned the system failing him, failing the people who needed him. She hadn't really understood that until now.

But Cassie held all that inside. "I'll be looking forward to the looks on your faces when you discover the real leak." Her tight smile disappeared. "In the meantime, the death of every single girl in the hands of those traffickers will be on you."

She rose from her chair. "So, sleep well knowing the chaos you've created in Boone County. And get yourselves a good representative. By the time I'm done, you'll be lucky if you're directing traffic in a one-stoplight town." She was bluffing, but she didn't intend to go down without a fight. It wasn't just about her. It was about the office of sheriff. It was about her father's legacy.

Cassie slapped her gun and badge on the desk and strode out of her office, head high, insides roiling with shame and frustration, and her right palm damp with blood. She'd failed her father. Her town. Her county. She had followed the rules. Adhered to protocol. And still, they were able to kick her out the door as if she were dirt on the bottom of their boots.

She reached Helen's desk and asked her in a low voice, "Have they questioned you yet about the leak?"

Helen nodded. "I'm not supposed to tell you anything. They said I'd be out on my butt if I did."

Cassie stared into Helen's eyes, but Helen remained silent. "So you're *not* going to tell me?"

"I didn't think you'd want me to. They were adamant about it, and I know how you feel about any of us doing what we're not supposed to."

Cassie felt the rigid strings that she lived by tug at her from every corner of her life. Going by the book hadn't helped her plug the leak, stop the traffickers, track down her father's killer or find Bishop's niece. Maybe the Rangers had done her a favor after all. Maybe now she would try it Bishop's way instead.

Placing her elbows on the desk, Cassie leaned down. "What if I told you they relieved me of duty, and maybe I'm going to do things differently for once?"

Helen's eyes went round. "They fired you?"

"I think it's more of a suspension-type thing."

"That's just not right." Her face crumpled and she grabbed a tissue. "How could they do that?"

"Pull it together, Helen. We're the ones who keep this place running with spit and baling wire. Remember?"

Helen nodded as she wiped her nose. "They only asked me if I'd seen any evidence of corruption in the department. I told them no. And that's the truth."

Cassie straightened and patted Helen's shoulder. "I'll keep in touch. We'll straighten everything out. Oh, and if you get a hit on that BOLO, call me. No one else." She walked out of the building, a plan already forming in her mind. She pulled out her phone as she reached her vehicle and hit speed dial.

"Bishop."

"Meet me back at the Pugh house. We need to talk."

Chapter Eighteen

Bishop stood in the doorway of the Pugh master bedroom, watching Cassie put Garrett's drugs and guns in a duffel bag. "I thought you couldn't do that 'cause it went against the rules."

"Yeah, well, I'm done playing by the rules." She opened the bottom dresser drawer, retrieved the baggie of cocaine and tossed it into the duffel.

"Any particular reason?" If it were true, Bishop sure wouldn't complain. But this just wasn't the Cassie he'd gotten to know.

She placed the handgun in the duffel, too, staring into the bag before her somber gaze met his. "Because doing everything by the book just got me relieved of duty. I'm no longer sheriff, and all I was doing was my job."

"Did they tell you why?"

"Whoever gave the Rangers false info about the leak is tipping them off about my actions, claiming it all ties into the trafficking case. Which I was ordered to stay clear of. And I have been."

"What leak?" Had he missed something?

"I meant to tell you about it the day after the Chute. By the time I got home from the hospital I forgot."

Bishop crossed his arms. "You sure you weren't still holding out on me?"

"Look, *Mister* Bishop, we need to get a few things straight if we're going to keep working together."

"Are we?" he asked, surprised she'd want to after his actions this morning. "Still working together, that is," he added when Cassie looked confused.

"You don't want to?" She backed up a step.

Bishop sighed. "Yes. I want to work together."

Cassie narrowed her eyes. "Even though you accused me of letting Garrett get away?"

"Getting him to confess was my best chance of finding Ashley alive. I had a right to be angry. Even now, his fingers itched to curl in on themselves.

"Next time you get mad, meditate or something, will you?"

Bishop snorted and ran a hand through his hair. "Yeah, yeah. Are you going to tell me about the leak?"

She dropped the bag. "We've figured there's been a leak related to the human trafficking case for quite a while. They were always one step ahead of us when we went after them." Cassie paced in the small room. "The Rangers arrived already knowing about the leak, said they were looking at everyone in my department."

"How'd they find out about it?"

"They said they couldn't reveal their source. Thing is, the only people they're looking at are my brothers and me. Oh, and my dad, if you can believe it." She snorted. "I know no one in my family is the leak, but unless we find the real culprit, Adam and Noah could wind up behind bars. And when the Rangers kicked us off the trafficking case, they made it clear they wouldn't be working it."

Bishop closed his eyes and took a calming breath. "Let me get this straight. No one is actively looking for the girls? Or the traffickers?"

"Nope. Not until now." She squared up to him, hands on hips, looking like the feisty Cassie he'd met on day one. "*Now*, you and I are going to be looking for them."

"How do you propose we do that? Especially since Garrett's gone."

"I put out a BOLO on his car." Cassie's lips curled into a very satisfied smile. "My last official act as sheriff."

"Nice move." Bishop started to smile but stopped. "If you're not in the office, though—"

"Already handled. I told Helen to call me, and only me, when there's a sighting." She picked up the duffel. "Let's go back to my house, figure out our plan."

Bishop allowed himself a moment to appreciate Cassie's resilience. "Why are you taking this stuff now? You can't turn it in as evidence."

"Like you said earlier, keep it out of Garrett's hands if he comes back here." Cassie winced when she shifted the bag. "Might even get him into trouble with whoever he's working for."

"Ribs still hurt?" Bishop didn't wait for her to respond but took the bag from her. She opened her mouth, probably to argue, but snapped it shut.

"Thanks." It was soft and hard to hear, but she said it all the same. And with that one word he followed her out of the room, hoping that this time, just maybe, their teaming up would work.

"They twinge every now and then, but don't worry. They won't slow me down."

"Not worried in the least." He raised a brow. "They didn't seem to slow you down last night."

Cassie shot him a look as a pink flush crept up her cheeks. "I only let you take my bag so I can save my energy for the bad guys." She stalked out of the house without looking back.

"Let's sit outside. It seems to be cooling off." Now if only Cassie could. Last night she'd felt more intimate with Bishop than she'd thought possible. His consideration, his gentleness, his passion had made her realize the difference between having sex and making love. *Better late than never.*

But today had given her doubts. He'd betrayed

her trust, and that was something hard to get past. If there even was any getting past it.

"Probably that front they predicted. Supposed to get some heavy rain with it." Bishop carried a dining room chair out with him. "Nice that your patio's covered."

"Grab another chair if you need to elevate your knee."

"It's practically good as new. But don't worry." He gave her a sly smile. "I'm saving my energy for the bad guys."

"Touché."

"How likely is it we'll get a hit on the BOLO soon?" Bishop stretched his legs out in front of him. "I mean, in this part of Texas?"

"Oh, us country bumpkin cops tend to ignore BOLOs. We just stand around at the corner gas station, drinkin' Cokes and talkin' 'bout how hot it is."

Bishop's lips twisted into a crooked smile. "You know what I meant."

"Actually, it's pretty likely," she said. "A lot of the towns around here don't get much excitement on a daily basis. So when a BOLO goes out, the police departments jump on it like a duck on a june bug."

His smile faded. "I feel like I should be doing something. Not just sitting here, waiting."

"Think of it as a stakeout. It's basically the same thing, except we're not in a car." Cassie leaned back in her chair. "When I'm on one with a deputy, we talk."

"Mine are always solo."

"You're not solo now. What do you want to talk about?"

"You."

Cassie scoffed. "We've already talked plenty about me. I want to hear why you quit the police force to become a PI."

Darkness spread across Bishop's face, and Cassie realized this wouldn't be an amusing story. But she wanted to hear it. She wanted to learn about the hidden parts of him that defined his character. She needed to understand what made a man who had once upheld the law become a man who thought himself above the law. So she waited him out.

"There was this kid, Jessica Santos. Nineteen, trying to save money for beauty school. Her boyfriend had talked her into doing a drug sale for him, said he'd give her a cut of the money that would pay her tuition in full." Bishop's tone foreshadowed where the story was going. "Instead, she wound up face-to-face with me in an interrogation room."

He stared out across her yard, his mind probably replaying the past.

"I believed her story. No priors, just bad choices when it came to men. The current boyfriend had a rap sheet a mile long but was free and clear on this bust. It ate at me that she'd be in prison and he'd still be on the street dealing drugs." He shook his head, as if regretting his next move. "So I gave her a chance to reclaim her life. Become my confidential informant, help me take down the boyfriend and the high-level connections above him, and she'd walk away with no charges, no jail time. She agreed."

A beat of silence followed and Cassie wondered if he'd continue. Finally, he blinked, breaking his stare and looking at her, a veil of sorrow dropping over his features. Something only a fellow officer might recognize.

Bishop swallowed. "Within a month, she was dead."

Cassie reached out a hand. "Bishop…"

He pulled back, as if her touch would weaken his resolve to keep talking. She understood.

"I'd given her a plausible cover story to explain why we released her, and she went back to her boyfriend. She let me know when he set up a meeting with his suppliers and she convinced him to take her along. Told him she wanted to make up for the last time, to learn enough that she could help him more in the future. When he agreed, we put a wire on her for the meet."

He continued, this time his eyes focused on his boots. "The operation was already in motion when a DEA agent called foul. One of their guys was undercover in the organization, and they were after the international dealers. My captain called off the op, but it was too late for Jessica."

Cassie reached out her hand again and this time he allowed her to rest it on his.

"We heard her scream when they found the wire. We were only a block away, but we couldn't go in because of our captain's order. I tried to anyway. I didn't care if I got fired as long as Jessica was safe. But my partner held me back until we heard a gunshot. When we arrived at the scene everyone was gone except the boyfriend. He was lying on the ground, dead from a bullet to the forehead."

Bishop's gaze met Cassie's. "A homeless man found her body in an alley dumpster. Medical examiner said she'd been sexually assaulted multiple times and shot up with uncut heroin."

Though not surprised, Cassie released a sigh of empathy.

"I was already tired of dealing with bureaucratic red tape on a daily basis. When that op was shut down, when Jessica's body wound up in the morgue, I completely lost it."

"What happened?"

"I blew up at my captain, his boss, the whole system. But it had about as much impact as water splashing against a rock. I knew nothing would change. So I turned in my gun and badge. I was done following the letter of the law, especially when it got innocent kids killed."

"I'm so sorry," Cassie whispered. Such a heartbreaking end to both a young woman's life and a good man's career. "Is that when you decided to go private?"

He let out a breath. "Not exactly. First, I drank too much. Yelled too much. Got into fights with strangers in bars and the next day couldn't even remember what the fights were about. I lost my career, my pride and my dignity so fast, it didn't take long to hit rock bottom." Bishop grimaced. "Then I quit drinking and started the anger management stuff. I tried to figure out what was next for me. I interned at my buddy's agency, liked it, and *that's* when I went private." He smiled a sheepish grin. "I've never told anyone that before."

Cassie's throat tightened with an emotion she couldn't identify. Bishop could have refused to answer her question. Instead, he'd allowed her a glimpse of those demons she'd wondered about. His anger when she insisted on going by the book now made more sense. "Thank you for telling *me*."

Bishop's eyes softened and he traced a finger along the inside of her arm. "Thank you for asking."

Her phone interrupted the moment. "Sher— Reed." How long before she'd stop saying "sheriff" when she answered?

"Hey, Cassie. It's Steve, from Winston."

"Hi, Steve. What's up?" Winston had its own police force, and Cassie had worked with their chief several times.

"Calling about that BOLO on the yellow Mustang."

Cassie straightened in her chair. "Yeah?"

"It sounded familiar. I'd seen one over in Hud
sonville a couple months back. So I took a littl
drive this evening, and sure 'nuff, it's parked b
the same house as before."

"The plates match?" Nervous energy jolted he
system.

"Wouldn't have called if they didn't. Want th
address?"

She pulled up her phone's notes app. "Go ahead.
After typing it, she read it back.

"That's it. It's an old farmhouse, 'bout a mil
from town. The car's empty, but the owner's mos
likely in that house. I know it's out of my jurisdic
tion, but if you want me to—"

"No!" When Bishop jumped in his seat, sh
could only imagine how surprised Steve was
"Sorry, didn't mean to yell, but no. We don't wan
him to know he's been found."

Steve chuckled. "Alrighty, then. Long as you'
be up here directly, I'll mosey on home."

"Thanks, Steve. I owe you one."

Cassie ended the call and looked at Bishop. "He'
in Hudsonville."

A predatory gleam lit his eyes. "Where's that?

"About twenty-five miles northwest of here." Sh
jumped to her feet. "I have to grab my person
gun. I'll meet you out front."

Bishop followed suit, eagerness radiating fror
him like the sun's heat at high noon. "We need t

swing by my room. I have to grab my other gun and more ammunition." He threw her a pained expression. "I suppose you're driving again?"

"Since mine's county-issued, I think we better take yours."

He let loose an exaggerated sigh of relief. "Great. I was afraid we'd still be on our way tomorrow if you drove."

"WHAT'S THE ADDRESS? I'll use my GPS." Bishop had zipped in and out of his motel room, and they were approaching the town limits.

"No need. I know exactly where it is. The fastest way is Highway 111." Cassie picked up a plastic grocery bag he'd tossed on the front console. "What's in here?"

"Protein bars. I don't know about you, but I'm hungry." He followed the road they were on to an intersection.

"This is 111. Turn right." She pulled the bars out of the bag. "You want one?"

"Please." He held his hand out toward her, but Cassie opened the wrapper and pulled it down partway before handing it to him. That was something different. And nice. He usually just ripped it open with his teeth. "Help yourself." He glanced at her wrinkled nose and skeptical look. "They taste like fudge brownies."

"Nothing that's good for you can possibly taste

like a fudge brownie." She tossed them back in the bag. Then her stomach rumbled.

"Sounds like someone disagrees with you." Bishop smirked. "At least try one. If you hate it, I'll finish it for you."

Cassie reached back into the bag and pulled out a bar. She tore it open and sniffed. "Hmph. Passes the smell test." She nibbled on the end of it.

Bishop's eyes on the road, he smiled wider as she ripped at the wrapper and chewed with enthusiasm.

"Okay. I didn't hate it. Therefore, it must not be healthy."

Chuckling, Bishop said, "If your hypothesis is based on faulty logic, your findings bear no validity."

Cassie turned her head and watched his profile. "Pretty face *and* smart? Who'da thunk?"

Bishop choked on his protein bar. "You think I'm pretty?" He glanced at her.

Cassie rolled her eyes. "Don't let it go to your head. I usually run as fast as I can from men with pretty faces."

"So, I'm an exception?" He laughed at Cassie's expression.

"Enough with pretty." Cassie leaned back against her seat, like they were two people just out for a drive. "Let's get back to smart. I'm even more impressed because I had to drop logic, statistics and physics in college. My brain is just not wired for that stuff."

"I only remember bits and pieces of it." Bishop passed a car going the precise speed limit, which made him even more thankful Cassie let him drive.

"Where'd you go to school?"

"Sam Houston. Majored in criminal justice. Got my master's in criminology."

"Wow. Not a lot of cops go for their graduate degree." She nodded, a look of approval on her face. "And here I thought you were just a cowboy who wanted to be a cop."

"A little more complicated, but that pretty much sums it up."

"Take a left up here." Cassie pointed. "Why was it complicated?"

"Just family stuff." Bishop made the turn. "Why are you so interested all of a sudden?"

"I told you about my family." She shrugged. "I want to hear about yours. Now spill."

Giving up, Bishop sighed. "Bob was always the golden child. Firstborn, good grades, college scholarships, high-paying job already lined up before he graduated." Bishop passed another car. "It's not that I was jealous of him. Even though he's quite a bit older than me, we were close. But it meant I'd eventually take over running the ranch. Didn't matter what I wanted."

"Which was to become a cop?"

Bishop nodded. "I'd told my folks that over and over for years. They either weren't listening or didn't care. One day, I was a senior in high school, my old man told me not to worry about getting a scholarship like Bob. Said he'd foot the bill for business school, which I'd need to run the ranch." Bishop sneered. "It was like he didn't know my grades were as good as my brother's. I'd already been approved for an academic scholarship, and I'd applied to several colleges."

"Did you tell him that?"

"I didn't get a chance to. I explained again that I had no intention of running the ranch for the rest of my life. That I was becoming a cop, and that was that." Bishop scoffed. "So he threw me out. Tossed my clothes through the window, locked the door and never spoke to me again."

"Wait, what? While you were still in high school?"

Cassie's indignant expression on his behalf warmed Bishop's heart. He'd learned not to reveal much of himself to people. It was the best way to avoid disappointment. But it seemed the more Cassie knew about him, the *less* she judged him. And vice versa. Day one, he'd pegged her as an uncompromising Goody Two-shoes that he wanted nothing to do with. And now? He wanted *everything* to do with her. He just needed to figure out what Cassie wanted.

"I stayed with a friend and his family until I graduated. By then I'd been accepted to the schools where I'd applied. With the scholarship and a part-time job, I could afford to live in the dorm for the first two years. I'd finished the forty-eight hours of class credits I needed to apply with HPD by then, but I figured I might as well keep on going. I shared an apartment with three other guys while I completed my junior and senior years."

"And graduate school?" She seemed completely enthralled with his life story.

"I was already a cop when I decided to go back for my master's."

"Huh." Cassie remained silent for a minute, apparently digesting his words. "What about your mom? Did she agree with your dad, or you?"

"My parents' marriage was based on Dad having everything his way and Mom never crossing him." He shrugged a shoulder. "Bob and I stayed close until a couple years ago, when he remarried. He kept Mom updated on what I was up to, but she wouldn't go behind my dad's back for even a phone call."

Bishop stopped at a light and looked over at Cassie, a thoughtful expression on her face. "Hey, it's fine. I couldn't care less what anyone thinks about my career choices. Not the one to become a cop, and not the one to quit the force. Sometimes you just have to do what's right for *you*. For your health, mental, physical and emotional. Stress can kill you."

Cassie flinched, as though he'd just struck a nerve. A car behind them honked, and she jumped in her seat. "Take a right here. The house is a few miles down the road."

Chapter Nineteen

Cassie strained to see Garrett's Mustang through the windshield. The drizzle that had started during the drive had become a steady rain. She pointed. "There, by the side of the house. See it?"

Bishop slowed to a crawl in the dark. "Barely. By that white truck?" With no traffic on this stretch of road, their headlights would have announced their approach. Bishop had turned them off a mile back. He stopped across from the house.

"That's probably the box truck they used in Resolute. I won't know for sure until I get closer." She muttered a curse under her breath. "I figured if just the Mustang was here, we'd only have to worry about Garrett, maybe one other guy. But with the truck here, too, I'm not sure how many might be inside." Cassie bit her lip.

"They might keep it here because the place is so isolated. Doesn't necessarily mean there will be more guys in there." He tapped his fingers on the steering wheel. "You thinking of calling for backup?"

Cassie met his questioning look. "That would be the smart thing to do if it weren't so complicated. If my brothers or Lonnie get involved, it could cost them everything. Same with my other three deputies. Or it could cost *us* everything if one of those other three happens to be the leak." She pinched the bridge of her nose. "And then there's the fact that I can't officially request backup since I'm not acting as sheriff."

"I'd rather keep it just the two of us, anyway." Bishop rubbed the back of his neck. "The more people in there firing guns, the better chance one of the girls gets killed."

Cassie gave him credit for not making it just about Ashley, even though she was the reason he was here. "We'll hold off on calling anyone. Worse comes to worst, I'll call Lonnie or Adam."

Bishop gave her a single nod of agreement.

"They sure picked a good location." Bishop drifted farther along until he found a wide spot on the shoulder about a hundred yards from the property. "Can't get much more isolated than this."

"It works in *our* favor, too. They won't be able to see us coming." She leaned forward in her seat and looked up at the gray sky. "Just wish the weather was better."

The storm had picked up quickly. Torrential rain now fell, and small trees bent under the force of the wind. Thunder roared simultaneously with a crack of lightning directly overhead.

Bishop reached into the back seat and brought up two folded packages. "Rain ponchos. I always keep extra." He handed one to Cassie.

She grinned. "Don't tell me you were a Boy Scout, too." She unfolded one of the black plastic ponchos and slipped it over her head.

"Nope. Learned this one the hard way." Bishop unwrapped the other one and pulled it on. "You want to split up, or stay together?"

"Let's decide when we get there. Be careful. The place in Resolute had security cameras, back and front. We can't lose the element of surprise." Cassie pulled her poncho's hood up and as far forward as she could, tying the plastic strips beneath her chin. "Your inside lights all turned off?"

"Yep. PI rule number one." He looked at her, his eyes as stormy as the weather. "Ready?"

She gave him a tight nod, her lips pressed together. They climbed out of the truck, eased their doors shut, and ran toward the farmhouse, their jeans, from the knees down, soaked in seconds.

As they reached the edge of the property, they stopped, huddling behind wind-whipped bushes. Cassie tucked her head down and took a few water-free gasps of air. Then she put her mouth right next to Bishop's ear. "Let's check out the truck."

She took point, running in a crouch. Stopping behind trees and foliage along the way, she watched for motion lights and movement near the house. They made it to the truck and checked both sides.

"There's no signage on it now, but this is the one they used in Resolute." Cassie pointed at the damaged rear bumper.

"We need to assume they have more than two men in there." Half of Bishop's words floated away on the wind.

Cassie pointed to herself, then the rear of the house. She tapped Bishop's chest and pointed back the way they'd come, indicating he should circle the house from the other side. With a single nod, he took off, and she hightailed it to the closest side of the building.

Squinting into the rain, Cassie scanned for security cameras but found none. She eased past windows covered by curtains and shades, pausing by each, straining to hear voices. If there were any, they were drowned out by the storm.

When she reached the back corner of the house, she stood with her back flat against the wall and took a quick peek around it. Still no security cameras, so she slid around and moved toward a window near the back door.

The door opened and Cassie froze, her chest too tight to breathe. Unintelligible voices came from inside, and the door swung closed with no one coming out. Unwilling to take a chance, she ran back the way she'd come, then circled through the trees until she stood behind a chicken coop. From her vantage point she had a clear view of the entire back of the house.

The door swung in again, and this time a man came out on the covered stoop with a lit cigarette. He wore a poncho like hers, and after a minute he pulled up his hood, turned on a flashlight and began a patrol of the property.

Saying a silent prayer that Bishop wouldn't be caught off guard, Cassie pulled off her poncho, balled it up and shoved it under a log. With the wind whipping it up against her face, it hadn't kept her dry, and she could move faster without it. As soon as the man rounded the far corner of the house, she ran back to the window. The curtains on this one hung crooked, and she looked through the gap. Two men, neither one Garrett, crossed her line of sight. *At least three inside, one outside.*

She caught movement in her peripheral vision and spun toward it, hand on her gun. Bishop moved at an angle toward her and a large barn a good ways back from the house. With frantic gestures, he urged her to run, and she did. A beam of light cut across her path and she slid behind the chicken coop.

"Hey!" The light bobbed as the man ran toward her. A gun had replaced his cigarette. "Get out here."

The rain had slacked off enough that Cassie could just barely make out his words. She crouched lower, willing her breathing to slow, and pulled her gun. Boots slogging through mud came closer. Peeking through a cracked board, she watched the man stop, hold up his light and lean forward. His flashlight hit the ground and his gun came up. Cassie dropped flat in the mud as a bullet buzzed past her.

Another shot, this one from Bishop on her left. Then a grunt, and she poked her head up in time to see the guard fall.

"You okay?" Bishop's yell reached her just as the back door flew open and at least six men rushed out.

"So far. You?"

"Yep. Stay down and watch for your chance." Then he disappeared behind the barn.

The men spread out across the yard, all of them armed with shotguns or handguns. None of them bothered to check on the guy Bishop had shot.

"There. Behind the barn." One of the men fired his shotgun toward Bishop's position.

The others joined in, and Cassie took advantage of the distraction Bishop had created for her. She filled her lungs with air and dashed for the front of the house, staying hidden behind foliage as much as possible. Reaching the front door, she listened for the gunfight. Bullets still flew back there.

Cassie tested the doorknob, but it was locked. *Here goes nothing.*

She raised her leg and kicked the door with the sole of her boot. It needed one more kick before it crashed inward. With her gun at the ready, she crept through the downstairs rooms. Empty. Cassie started up the stairs, cringing with every creak of the boards beneath her feet.

The bedrooms were upstairs. She eased open one door and experienced an unwelcome sense of déjà vu. Wall-to-wall mattresses, two girls on each. One leg of each girl was cuffed to a large bolt in the floor by a zip tie. Cassie flipped the light switch and a dim bulb came on. She crouched next to the closest girl and examined her ankle. It was red and raw from the plastic tie.

She moved to the other end of the mattress and felt for a pulse. Thready, but there. The girl's eyes were rolled back in her head, with only the whites showing. Cassie checked each girl on each mattress. Some moaned and looked at her with vacant expressions. Some were out cold. A few raised limp hands to her, begging for more dope.

"I'll be back soon to free you all." The gunfight in the backyard still raged on and she had to make sure the girls didn't stumble into more harm.

As Cassie moved from room to room, each one like the last, the depravity of these evil monsters filled her with stone-cold fury. She repeated her promise to each group of girls as she went. She found Ashley in the third room, near the door. Cassie dropped to her knees and checked her vitals. Alive, but unconscious. She brushed the girl's snarled hair back from her face. "Your Uncle Tyler is here, Ashley. *We're* here." As though Ashley could understand her, she rolled her head toward Cassie and moaned.

A creak outside the door brought Cassie to her feet, spinning toward the sound. Garrett froze in the hall, then took off down the stairs. Cassie followed, catching up with him in the middle of the living room. She raised her gun.

"Don't make me do it." She clenched her jaw in anger. "And don't doubt that I will. On the floor."

Spitting out a string of curse words, he lay down on his stomach and put his arms behind his back.

"So glad you're familiar with the position." Cassie looped a zip tie around his wrists and tightened it. "I think I'll play it safe this time." She cuffed his ankles together, then searched him, removing two pocketknives and small amounts of drugs. "Staying true to form, aren't you? I bet the minute the shooting started, you hid upstairs. I'd think it would be downright embarrassing getting caught running away every single time."

He mumbled something, but with his mouth against a filthy braided rug, it was hard to understand and she really didn't care. Leaving him prone on the floor, Cassie went to the back door. Only two of the traffickers still stood. She let out a shrill whistle and when they turned toward her, Bishop came out from behind the barn.

"Time to lay 'em down, boys." She raised her gun in a two-handed grasp. "You're surrounded."

One started to swing his gun toward her, and

Bishop called out, "Uh-uh-uh. You'll be dead before you pull the trigger."

Both men looked from Cassie to Bishop, dropped their guns and raised their hands. Bishop made quick work of the zip ties while Cassie held her gun on them. He herded them to the back door, and Cassie pulled two kitchen chairs around while Bishop frisked them. Then they cuffed their ankles to the legs and their already-cuffed hands to one of the back slats on the chair.

"No more inside?" Bishop asked.

"Just one. He's in the living room, trussed up like a Thanksgiving turkey." She met his hopeful eyes. "She's upstairs. Second bedroom to the right."

Bishop was gone before the last word crossed her lips.

BISHOP TOOK THE stairs two at a time. He raced past the first room, skidding to a stop at the second door. Steeling himself, he looked in at a horror he would never forget.

There, on a filthy mattress she shared with another girl, he found Ashley. Bishop dropped to his knees and took her limp body in his arms. Her head lolled to the side as he brushed back her hair.

"Ashley, can you hear me?"

A low moan escaped her lips, but her eyes remained closed. Bishop laid her back down, noticing needle tracks on the inside of her elbow. He dropped his head into his hands, fighting back tears. "I'm sorry, Little Turtle. I'm sorry it took me so long to find you." Raising his head and scrubbing at his cheeks, he pulled out his pocketknife and sliced through the zip tie cutting into her ankle.

"You're safe now, Ash. I'm getting you out of here." He cradled her in his arms, about to stand, when he looked across the room. Every one of these young women had someone searching for her. Before he could save any of them, even Ashley, there was something he needed to do.

Kissing Ashley's forehead, he rested her on the mattress. Then he stood, curled his hands into fists, and welcomed back the old Bishop.

Cassie was halfway up the stairs when he stormed past her. "What's wrong?" Her footsteps followed him down.

Bishop strode to Garrett, picked him up by his cuffed arms and jerked him to his feet. "You're gonna pay, you little—"

"Is Ashley…she's still alive, right?" Cassie asked from behind him.

"Oh, she's alive. But this piece of garbage doped her almost all the way to death's door. She has needle tracks in her arm and can't even open her eyes." Bishop drew his gun and pointed it at Garrett's chest. He allowed his anger to take control, and it flowed through him, pumping in sync with his blood. In the past, alcohol had been the middleman. Now, sober, he realized the full power of his fury.

"What are you doing? You can't shoot him in

cold blood." Cassie stepped next to Bishop. "Let the legal system handle him."

"We've both seen how well the system works. Jessica Santos is dead, and you're not wearing your badge."

Another round of rain pounded the roof and thunder rumbled. Cassie slipped between the two men, facing Bishop. "This isn't you. It's not the Bishop who meditates, does deep breathing, centers his chi."

"Get out of my way, Cassie." Bishop didn't lower his gun.

"I said I'd try things your way. And you were right. Bending the rules works sometimes." Her eyes pleaded with him. "But I will not allow you to cross this line. Look, I called Lonnie. He'll be here soon. Let him handle Garrett."

"You won't shoot me." Garrett lifted his chin, his mouth twisted into a smug grin. "Didn't last time, won't this time."

Bishop steadied his gun with both hands. "I owe it to Ashley."

"This is the last thing Ashley would want you to do." Cassie rested a hand on his arm, and he shook it off. "Bishop, she has a chance to recover. You think she will if you're in prison because of her?"

At her words, Bishop blinked, the first seed of doubt in his actions creeping in. But he doubled down on his rage, clenching the gun tighter. "You're not a sheriff. You have no say about it."

"I'm not saying this as a sheriff, Bishop. I'm saying this as the woman who's falling in love with you."

"Cassie…" An unfamiliar hitch in Bishop's chest had him relaxing his grip. The previous flames of fury died down to manageable embers.

"You do this," she continued, her hand now resting over his heart, "you'll never come back from it. You'll lose yourself for good. *I'll* lose you for good."

It was the break in Cassie's voice that was his final undoing. He couldn't do this to her, or Ashley, or even himself. He was better than this.

Bishop took a deep breath, exhaled and lowered his gun. Breaking away from the terrified gaze of Garrett Pugh, he met Cassie's loving green one and dropped his head forward on her shoulder.

"You should listen to her," Lonnie said, walking in from the kitchen.

Bishop only had time to raise his head when a searing pain shot through it. *This is getting really old.* And he surrendered to the blackness.

"Lonnie, no! That's Bishop!" Cassie dropped to the floor and took his head in her hands, a sticky wetness turning them red.

"Oops. My mistake." Lonnie slipped his gun into his waistband, bent over and wrapped an arm around Cassie's waist, pulling her to her feet. At the same time, he yanked her gun from its holster and tossed it on a chair. Dragging Cassie along, he cut the zip ties that bound Garrett.

"You really are useless, aren't you?" Lonnie yelled at him. "First you kill that girl in Resolute, and now—" he waved his gun around "—all this."

"Hey, none of this is my fault."

"*Everything* is your fault!" Lonnie yelled right to Garrett's face. "None of this would have happened if you hadn't grabbed his niece." Then he spoke as if addressing a child. "Now, pick up his gun, Garrett. Then pick up the gun on the chair. Try not to kill anybody and keep an eye on this dirtbag." He kicked Bishop in the side. "Do you think you can do that?"

Nodding, Garrett scrambled to get both guns and out of Lonnie's way.

Cassie struggled against Lonnie's hold while her mind fought to make sense of what was happening. "You're part of this?"

"I'm so glad you called me, my poor, confused cousin. See, I'm the one they ask for when there are messes to clean up. And whooee, coz, you made quite the mess."

The barrel of a gun touched the side of Cassie's head and her blood ran cold. Inhaling a deep breath, she forced herself to stay calm, ready for a chance to break free. "Why would you do it?"

"You mean work with these guys? Come on, Cass. You think I make enough money as a deputy to support my gambling? I was in debt up to my eyeballs before I started helping them out." He took a step back toward the door, pulling her with him. "Or did you mean the sad end of Wallace Reed?"

Cassie gasped and wrestled against his grip, but he held her too tight. "You killed Dad?"

"He wasn't *my* dad. Y'all never treated me like anything other than an outsider." He stepped back again. "And it was worse at the office. I worked there for years before you, but who gets to be chief deputy? Figured killing him would take care of two birds at the same time. He was getting way too close to figuring out I was tipping off the traffickers. Plus, thought for sure I'd be moved into his position. *And* his paycheck." He chuckled. "Oh well. One out of two ain't bad."

Garrett dropped onto the couch and sneered at Cassie as Lonnie jerked her through the doorway. He dragged her backward toward the trees, both of them slipping in the mud. The rain felt like pebbles against her skin, and its roar drowned out all other sound.

Cassie shifted her weight against him, throwing him off balance, and Lonnie slid down to one knee, still holding on to her. Cassie raised her right leg, then swung it back as hard as she could. Lonnie screamed, and she knew she'd hit what she'd been aiming for. She lurched from his grasp, saw his gun on the ground and scrabbled her way toward it.

He grabbed her ankle as her fingers touched the barrel. She twisted and clawed at the mud, but he held tight and pulled her away from it. Flipping her onto her back, he hauled off and punched her in the jaw.

"That the best you can do?" She spit blood in his face and jabbed her thumbs into his eyes.

Lonnie rolled off her, his hands covering his eyes. Cassie jumped to her feet and ran to the gun. She held it in both hands, aiming straight at Lonnie as he rose from the ground.

"You conniving piece of filth." Lightning slashed through the sky in a ragged line; the thunder that followed shook the earth. "How could you? I loved you like a brother." She dragged her hand across her face, wiping away the rain from her eyes. Rage like she'd never felt before erupted from her very soul.

Another flash of lightning revealed Bishop almost next to her, his gun drawn.

In the next flash, Lonnie reared up like a wounded grizzly, his face unrecognizable with hate and insanity as he rushed toward her.

Cassie shot him.

FLASHING BLUE AND red lights, along with the headlights of more emergency vehicles than Bishop thought existed in Boone County, lit up the night sky. The rain had tapered off, and he held Ashley's hand as two medics carried her stretcher to one of the ambulances. Still too doped up to speak, she gave his fingers a gentle squeeze from time to time.

He'd immediately texted his brother the good news about finding Ashley. Helping her recover came next. He wanted to ride with her to the hospital, but they were doubling up on patients in each ambulance and still making multiple trips.

"You won't be able to see her for a while anyway," the medic told him. "The docs are going to be busy tonight."

Bishop kissed Ashley's forehead. "I'll be there as soon as I can, Little Turtle. But you're safe now." He reached into his pocket, coming out with the turtle key chain he'd carried with him since learning Ashley was gone. He tucked it into her hand, curling her fingers around it.

"I already told you, I wasn't acting in the capacity of sheriff. How many times do I have to repeat myself before you get it?"

Bishop turned toward the aggravated voice. Cassie, a blanket around her shoulders, water still streaming from her hair, sat on the tailgate of his truck facing two tall men in Stetsons.

The Rangers had arrived.

Bishop walked over to stand next to Cassie, glad that she had told him enough about the two men to tell them apart.

"You need to step away, sir," Ward said. "We're conducting an interview."

"You're conducting it on my truck, and since I'm already here, I think I'll hang around. See what's what, if you know what I mean."

Cassie smiled when he threw Ward's own words from the Palmer murder back at him. Bishop returned her smile, the most beautiful thing he'd seen in hours.

"One more time, then we're done." She reached her hand out to Bishop's. "I came here as a private citizen, to help my friend find his niece."

"And leave a yard full of dead bodies," Ward deadpanned.

"Who were killed by legally registered guns while we were defending ourselves."

Mills jumped in. "Regardless of all that, we're going to need you to come down to the station and make a statement." He glanced at Bishop. "You, too."

"No problem." Cassie stood. "Oh, and you're welcome."

"For what?" Ward did not seem happy. Which seemed to make Cassie very happy.

"Oh, let's see. Finding your leak for you."

"Finding the traffickers for you," Bishop added.

"But the girls?" Cassie gazed into Bishop's eyes. "That was all him." She tilted her head as if pondering something. "Think I just might need to call the newspapers about that story."

Ward sputtered as Bishop closed the tailgate and walked Cassie to the passenger door. Before he opened it, he pulled Cassie close. "How are you doing?" He searched her face. "About Lonnie?"

Cassie closed her eyes for a moment. "I still can't

believe it." When she opened them, she looked more lost than he'd ever seen her. "I loved him. My dad loved him. How could he... How could I..." She trailed off, looking unblinking into the flashing lights of a retreating ambulance.

Bishop wrapped his arms tighter around her. " don't know, Cassie. But I do know this isn't on you Lonnie lied. Took advantage of your whole family. That's on him."

She sank into Bishop's side. "I just feel so be trayed."

"I understand. But he'll get what he deserves." Bishop kissed the top of her head. "By the way that was one heck of a shot."

Her lips twisted. "It would've felt good to shoo him in his thigh. Hit his femoral and watch him bleed out like he watched Dad." She sighed. "Bu I wanted to see him go to prison, too, so I figured I'd get even for my arm."

"I think you got more than even, consider ing your wound was a through-and-through." He chuckled.

"Yeah, blowing apart his rotator cuff was kind o a bonus." She was silent a moment, a smile on he face as if reliving the moment. But then it faded and her eyes focused on his. "Ward told me if the have to, they'll offer him a deal so he'll flip on th rest of the trafficking ring." She touched the bac of his head. "How's the noggin?"

"Sore." He smiled when she pulled her han

away. "Not *that* sore. Just glad Lonnie didn't hit me in the same spot that he did at Palmer's. I wasn't out long this time." He snorted. "And that idiot Garrett was in the kitchen looking for something to eat when I came to."

Cassie shook her head. "I'm sure he'll be charged with murder, no deals. He's too far down the food chain." She looked him straight in the eye, her brows pinched together. "How are you doing in here?" She patted his chest. "I can't imagine the mix of emotions."

"It's a lot," Bishop agreed. The image of his niece, lying stoned and half-dressed, would be branded on his mind for a long time. "I'm still angry. Probably always will be. But I'm more relieved that we found Ashley and that she'll be all right. At least physically."

Cassie tightened her hug. "She'll heal emotionally, too. Probably take a long time, but she's got you to help her."

They were silent for a while, content in the comfort they gave each other.

"Hey," he murmured against her hair. "You almost sounded proud of me back there, with the Rangers."

"Almost?" Cassie frowned. "I guess I should do better than that when I *show* you how proud I am." She leaned closer and whispered in his ear, "Because now I'm saving all my energy for the good guy."

Chapter Twenty

Marge had outdone herself with the pies. Cassie set both the cherry and the apple on the dining room table, since there wasn't a spot of empty counter space in the Reed kitchen.

Bishop's deep voice drifted in from the backyard, mingling with her brothers' laughter. Cassie smiled to herself. It sounded right.

Nate came in through the kitchen door. "Hey, sis." He went straight to the fridge and grabbed three beers. "Bishop is great. Glad you invited him to dinner." He disappeared back outside.

Cassie gathered the tequila, a shot glass and a bowl of lime wedges from the fridge. She tossed back a shot, steeling herself for the evening to come. It would be a night of family, laughter, good food. And through it all, she'd be rebuilding the wall around her heart. Protecting it for when she said goodbye to Bishop.

His career, his family, his life were in Houston. She scoffed. Less than a week ago, she was attracted to him because he was just passing through.

But then she went and fell in love with him. She'd even *told* him she loved him.

And he hadn't said it back.

She couldn't ask him to stay. Her pride couldn't take the rejection. Her heart couldn't withstand the crushing blow.

Cassie poured herself one more shot, forced her lips into a smile and went out to join the others.

Bishop, talking to Adam by the grill, glanced up as she came out on the patio. He smiled, and she couldn't help but smile back. Covering the space in a few strides, he hugged her and covered her mouth with his. Despite the twins' jeers and catcalls, the kiss seemed to last forever.

He led her to two patio chairs sitting close together. Very close together. As soon as they sat, he reached for her hand. "How'd it go with Frick and Frack after I left this morning?"

Cassie laughed at Bishop's on-the-nose nicknames for the Rangers. He'd gone in to give his statement in the morning, before spending the day at the hospital. "Well, before I met with them, I spoke with Michael Pugh. He was upset that the doctors wouldn't let him see Ashley. I told him he and Billy could stay in their house if he remains in Resolute."

"I hope he decided to stay," Bishop said.

"No, he's going back to Houston and taking Billy with him. He thinks he has a better future there."

"Not with Ashley, he doesn't." Bishop glared at her.

She raised her hands. "That's between Ashley, her family and her doctors."

"Hmph."

"Then I had to apologize to Dave. I'd suspected him unfairly. I needed to set that right."

"He didn't even know," Noah said. "I can't believe you apologized to that—"

"Enough, Noah. We're going to foster better relationships in the department from now on."

"You only suspected him because Lonnie fed you his line of—"

"And enough out of you, Nate. I thought I made it clear, we're not discussing our cousin tonight." She'd suffered enough at Lonnie's hands for too long. He'd killed her dad, tried to kill Bishop at Palmer's house and tried to kill her at least twice. She wanted an evening filled with good memories to hold close after Bishop was gone.

She forced her mind away from Bishop's leaving. "Once I did meet with Ward and Mills, it took a while to give them my statement. Then they tried to make me fill out all of *their* paperwork. I told them a private citizen can't do that."

"I bet they loved that," Adam said.

"First, they apologized for the huge misunderstanding. Then Mills said he'd worked a case with Dad years ago." She swallowed hard over a sudden lump in her throat. "Said he had nothing but respect for him and deep admiration for me."

"He had a nice way of showing it." Bishop stretched out his legs.

"Next, they said the county council had already reinstated me. Turns out my removal was provisional. Then Ward handed me my gun and badge."

"They're cagey, those two." Noah strolled by the grill to check on dinner.

"Not cagey enough." Cassie smirked. "I thanked him, told him as sheriff I forbid the practice of officers not filling out their own reports, and I left."

"Wish I'd been there to see his face." Noah knocked bottles with Adam and they drank.

While her brothers saluted her with beers, Cassie leaned closer to Bishop. "How's Ashley doing?"

His face clouded over. "The good news is that she wasn't assaulted."

Cassie's hand went to her heart. "You must be so relieved."

"You have no idea." His fingers curled and released.

"And the bad news?"

"They shot her up so many times, she's going through withdrawal." He shoved his fingers through his hair. "She'll be in detox for weeks. And then she'll most likely need help to heal emotionally."

"The poor thing. After what she already went

through, to have another ordeal ahead of her. Will you stay here while she's in the hospital?"

Bishop shook his head. "I explained all this to Bob, and he's planning to come down here tomorrow on his company's private jet. He'll fly her back to Houston as soon as the doctor releases her."

"Can she handle the flight in her condition?"

"Her doctor says yes, as long as Bob follows all his instructions to the letter." He shrugged. "I can't blame him. He's been worried sick about her since she ran off. If she were my daughter and I had a private jet, I'd do the same thing."

"I suppose her stepmom will be coming along?"

"I seriously doubt it. I was trying to find a tactful way to tell him that Ashley would need some time away from Monique. To decompress, successfully make it through withdrawal, stay clean. He said Ashley won't have to worry about Monica anymore." Bishop chuckled. "The highlight was him not calling her Monique."

Cassie forced a light laugh. "What about you? Are you going back with them?" Her right hand curled in on itself in her lap.

"I'm driving back. I told Bob I'd help get Ashley settled in." Bishop met her gaze. "I leave day after tomorrow."

She forced her eyes from his, afraid he'd see the silent pleading in them. At least she knew for sure. What they had, what she'd *thought* they had, was over. In two days he'd be gone, and she'd never see him again.

Her nails dug deep.

"Dinner's ready. Y'all come help yourselves." Adam carried platters of steak, chicken and vegetables to their patio table.

"You outdid yourself, bro." Nate pushed ahead of Noah and snagged the biggest steak.

As Cassie took in the special dishes made for Bishop, she met Adam's eyes and mouthed "thank you." He gave her a brotherly wink.

Bishop, coming along behind her, said, "Adam, you didn't have to go to all this trouble." He speared a chicken breast for his plate, then moved on to the vegetables. Grilled corn on the cob, asparagus, mushrooms and zucchini filled the platter.

"No trouble at all. Besides, this whole family needs more—"

"Don't say it," Nate and Noah chimed in unison.

"Vegetables," Adam finished.

Bishop sat next to Cassie at the table, and she poured him a glass of iced tea.

"No thanks. I'm fine. Maybe I'll just get some water." He pushed back his chair to stand.

"Try it. If you don't like it, I'll finish it for you." She gave him a teasing smile.

Bishop took a tentative sip, then shot a look of surprise Cassie's way. "This isn't sweet."

"That pitcher," Cassie said, and pointed to the one nearest him, "is just for you."

"And this," he said before he kissed her, "is jus for you."

"Good thing, 'cause none of us want to swap spit with you," Nate managed around a mouthfu of steak.

AFTER THE FOOD was eaten, the pies served and the dishes cleared, they sat around a firepit as the stars came out. Bishop watched Cassie avoid his eyes. Her smiles seemed forced, as if she'd tired of his company and was ready for him to be gone.

She'd told him she loved him, and he'd assumed she meant it. Her words had broken through his rage, banishing the Bishop who couldn't control himself. But in hindsight, she probably would have said anything to stop him from shooting Garrett. Probably best that Lonnie had knocked him out before he told her he loved her, too. Things were awkward enough between them now.

"Wow." He tipped back his head and stared at the sky. "Don't see stars like this in Houston."

Cassie looked up. "How can you stand to live where you can't see the stars?"

"I guess I just got used to it." He shrugged. "Same with sunrises. The tall buildings block the view."

Every Reed stared at him as if he'd said something blasphemous. "What?"

"No stars *and* no sunrises?" Noah scoffed. "That's just wrong."

"You need to get out of H-town, man." Nate tipped the neck of his beer toward Bishop. "Move down here where you can enjoy life."

All three Reed brothers nodded. But Cassie stared straight ahead at the fire, only her profile in view. She seemed to be the only Reed who didn't want him to return.

She stayed quiet while Bishop told PI tales, and Adam and Noah shared deputy adventures.

After a while, and a few hilarious stories later, Nate nudged her foot with his. "Cass, you've got the best ones of all. Contribute to the conversation, would ya?"

She stood, stretched and yawned. "I need to get going. It's been a long couple days, and I can barely see straight."

"I should go, too." Bishop rose next to her. "I'll walk you out." He moved around the fire, shaking each brother's hand. "Thanks for the invitation. Can't remember when I've enjoyed myself this much."

"Know how to solve that, don't ya?" Adam asked, brow raised.

In unison, both twins said, "Get your woo-woo self back down here as soon as you can."

Bishop gave Cassie the side-eye. "What have you been telling them?"

"Only the truth." She reached out her arms and wiggled her fingers. "Woo-woo." But this time, she didn't laugh along with her teasing words.

A few minutes later they stood next to her SUV.

"Any chance we can spend more time together before I leave?" Bishop wrapped his arms around her and rested his forehead against hers. "*Alone* time?"

"Tonight?" Her voice was soft, hesitant, as if she wasn't sure.

"I promised Ashley I'd sit with her tonight. She's scared of her own shadow." But Bishop kept trying, determined not to give up on them without a fight. "Tomorrow?"

"It's my first day back as sheriff. There's no way I can play hooky. What about tomorrow night?" Cassie pulled her head back, the invitation clear in her eyes.

His lips met hers, and they didn't stop until the sound of a brother's fake cough cut through the air, followed by the slam of the front door.

Chuckling, Bishop opened her car door for her. "Tomorrow night will be perfect."

CASSIE STAGGERED INTO her house, her arms full of shopping bags and packages. She'd been on the run since the minute she left work, determined to make this a night to remember. After sticking cold items in the fridge and the rest on her kitchen counter, she returned to the living room and started emptying bags on the couch.

She covered her coffee table with new, colorful place mats. From the largest bag she pulled out four huge, poufy pillows, each in a different color, and threw them haphazardly on the floor. Her eye started to twitch and she picked them up, setting them on the couch in a nice, orderly row. *Come on, Cass, you can do this.* She tossed them back on the floor around the table.

Back in the kitchen, she removed chopsticks and small dipping-sauce bowls from another bag. She set plates on two of the place mats, along with forks and chopsticks. She added the small bowls at intervals across the table.

Nodding with approval, she took a quick shower, then changed into leggings and a soft, loose tunic. A quick glance at the clock told her Bishop would be here soon. She dashed into the kitchen and pulled out all her purchases from the fridge. On the extra place mats she set out plates of sushi rolls and sashimi. She removed the top from the container of seaweed salad and sniffed it, wrinkling her nose. *Not so sure about this one.*

A bottle of unsweetened iced green tea filled two wineglasses. She added them to the place settings, then a bowl of undressed fruit salad for dessert. Cassie stood back and gave the table a critical once-over. She fought the urge to straighten the chopsticks, then gave in and lined them up along the edges of the mats. She'd just set low-sodium tamari sauce on the table and put dabs of wasabi and pieces of pickled ginger in the small bowls when the doorbell rang.

Bishop came in carrying a bottle of red wine. "I may not drink the stuff, but I know red goes better with beef."

"What makes you think I'm making steak tonight?" She maneuvered to block his view.

"Just a feeling." He managed to get past her and saw the coffee table. "I thought you refused to eat sushi? And sashimi?"

The happy look on his face set off a warm glow within Cassie. She shrugged. "Figured I can't say I don't like it unless I've actually tried it." She took his bottle of wine and set it in the kitchen.

He sneaked up from behind and wrapped his arms around her. When he left a trail of kisses down the side of her neck, she moaned at the hot chills racing across her body. Gasping, she pulled herself from his arms.

"We, uh, should probably eat." Cassie waved toward the living room. "I'm guessing there's a fine line between raw fish and food poisoning."

She took Bishop's hand and led him to the coffee table, then dropped down onto one of the floor pillows. She crossed her legs beneath her.

Bishop toed off his boots in the entry, then sat on the pillow next to her. "Before we start eating, I owe you an apology."

She cocked her head to the side as she met his eyes. "What for?"

"For treating you the way I did when Garrett got away. I'd lost control with him, and you stopped me from taking it too far." He ran his fingers through his hair, and Cassie's chest hitched, knowing how much she'd miss seeing that quirky habit of his. "I should have thanked you, instead of blaming you for his escape."

Cassie laced her fingers with his, noticing for the first time how right their hands looked together. "I appreciate your apology, and I forgive you." What she would never forgive him for was making her love him. "Now, how do you work these darn chopsticks?"

Bishop chuckled as he picked up the salad container. "Have you ever eaten seaweed salad?"

"Do you even have to ask me that?" She gave up on her chopsticks and used her fork to move a couple pieces of sushi onto her plate. "And don't be surprised if I never do."

"You have to try it. You said yourself you can't say you don't like it if…"

She pursed her lips at him. "It's green stuff from the bottom of the ocean."

"You'll love it." Bishop dished some of the salad onto her plate as she was about to slice a piece of sushi with her fork. He reached over and stopped her hand. "You just put the whole thing in, like this."

He demonstrated by filling his mouth with a piece of dragon roll. Sure that she'd hate it, Cassie picked up the smallest piece on the plate and popped it in her mouth.

But as she chewed, she was struck by the flavors exploding in her mouth. "What are the little things popping in there?" She pointed at her mouth.

"You like them?"

She nodded. "What are they?"

"Fish eggs."

Cassie paused in her chewing. She looked more closely at the piece still on her plate. She pointed at the tiny orange balls covering the top of it. "Those things?"

"Yep." Bishop took a swig of his green tea, but Cassie could see the smile in his eyes.

"Huh. They look like the salmon eggs we catch fish with." She looked at Bishop. "But they taste a heck of a lot better."

"You ate salmon egg bait?"

"Tried one when I was a kid. Once was enough."

"Then you can definitely give the salad a shot."

She picked up her fork and looped one tine under a thin thread of seaweed.

"You have to use your chopsticks."

Cassie perked up. "Seeing as I can't pick anything up with them, this shouldn't be too bad."

"I'll show you." Bishop scooted over and sat behind her. He reached around and picked up her chopsticks. After showing her how to hold them, he placed them in her hand and adjusted them. "Now you just move the top one, keeping the bottom one steady."

She tried, but the top one slid out of place. Bishop

took her hand in his and moved it to the salad. Together they picked some up with her chopsticks. He
slowly moved it to her mouth. She parted her lips
and Bishop set the bite of seaweed on her tongue.

Tentatively at first, she chewed the salad.

Bishop scooted around in front of her. "You like
it?"

Surprised by the fresh and nutty flavor of the
sesame oil dressing, she nodded as she swallowed
and licked her lips.

Bishop leaned in and kissed the corner of her
mouth. "Not so bad, expanding your horizons, is
it?"

"Since it's our last time together…" She blinked
at the burn behind her eyes and looked down. She
refused to ruin this night with the bittersweet tears
of a passionate goodbye.

Bishop lifted her chin until she met his earnest,
hopeful gaze. "I planned to ask you later, but…" A
sly grin curled his lips. "You think Boone County
could use a private investigator?"

Cassie's heart pounded from a whiplash of emotions. "Not sure about Boone County, but I know
the local sheriff could sure use one."

They leaned toward each other, meeting in the
middle with a kiss that took her breath away.

"Thank you for the amazing dinner," he murmured against her ear.

Cassie straightened her legs and wrapped them
around his waist. As Bishop lowered her back

against her pillow, she fisted her hands in his shirt, taking him with her.

"Well, you know what they say. The end justifies the means."

Epilogue

Three months later

Bishop grinned and looked at Cassie. "What do you think?"

The shiny new sign on the door read Bishop Investigations.

"*I* think you shoulda made it 'Discreet Inquiries' instead of 'Investigations,'" Marge said, standing on one side of Bishop while Cassie stood on the other side, admiring his new office. "Saw that on one of them English detective shows on TV. Sounded all sophisticated. 'Course, that many letters woulda cost you a goldurn arm and a leg."

"Well, *I* think it's perfect." Cassie beamed at him. "And it's mostly thanks to you, Marge."

"I didn't do nothin' 'cept spread the word about you two and your heroics. There's more'n one way to spice up the food at The Busy B." She cackled. "I bet you're glad to be out of Cassie's extra bedroom and into your own honest-to-goodness office."

"That, I am." Bishop tightened the arm he had around Marge.

"Hey." Cassie poked him in the side. "What's wrong with my extra bedroom?"

Marge stepped around Bishop and next to Cassie. "There's better uses for that room than runnin' a business." She gave Cassie a lewd wink, then slapped Bishop on the arm. "Catch my drift?"

Bishop chuckled. "Slow your roll, Marge. I think Cassie wants to stick to the traditional order of these things. Right?"

"Absolutely. Engagement, marriage and *then* babies. But I'm not in a rush." Cassie leaned against him. "In the meantime, we can turn it into a guest room. I'd love to have Ashley visit."

"I'd like that, too. But I don't think it will happen anytime soon." His niece had made it through detox, but was afraid to leave the house now. "Maybe we can take a road trip to Houston to see her."

"Whatever's best for her." Cassie smiled. "A visit from you would do her a world of good."

"Cassie, be a dear and walk back to the diner with me. It's almost time for the dinner rush, and my leg's been bothering me today."

"Of course, Marge. Do you want me to drive you back?"

"I'm not an invalid, for gosh sakes. I just want someone along in case I fall in the middle of the street. Don't wanna roll around like a turtle on its back until somebody runs over me."

Cassie took her arm and they started down the street. At the corner, Marge looked back and gave Bishop a thumbs-up. He returned the gesture, then jogged over to the justice center.

"Good afternoon, Helen." He stopped at her desk, waiting for permission to go past. It had become a game for them.

"Hello, Bishop. Ready for the big event?"

"Working on it. Adam and Noah here?"

"Go on back." She flashed him a smile. "And don't start without me."

"Wouldn't dream of it." He went to Adam's office first. "Can the chief deputy come out and play?"

"About time you got here." Adam checked his watch. "We're cutting it close."

"Then let's get going." They swung past the bullpen, picking up Noah.

"The rest of you guys," Adam addressed Sean, Pete and Dave, "be at the house at six o'clock sharp."

They saluted him and said in unison, "Yes, sir, Chief Deputy, sir."

"They still giving you a hard time about your promotion?" Bishop asked.

"Every day. But I get even with them because… I'm the chief deputy." They laughed as they climbed into Adam's truck. "We need to stop by your place, or pick up anything else?"

Bishop patted his pocket. "Got everything I need."

When they arrived at the Reeds' house, Bishop's jaw dropped. "Holy..."

"You might as well forget that phrase," Noah said. "My sister will wash your mouth out with soap."

Bishop climbed out of the truck and tried to take it all in. A dance floor had been set up in the front yard. Strings of little lights hung everywhere. Long tables for the food stood end to end near the front porch, and more were set up for drinks, both soft and hard.

Nate joined Bishop. "What do you think?"

"I can't believe it." A sudden panic swept through him. "What if she doesn't say yes? I should have done this privately. Not in front of half the town."

"Chill. She's going to say yes." Nate slapped his shoulder. "Go check out the backyard."

Bishop walked through the house, feeling at home. By falling in love with Cassie, he'd wound up with the type of family he had always wanted. He stepped out onto the patio to a rousing cheer from the crowd hiding back here.

He moved through, shaking hands and getting slapped on the back.

"'Bout time you put a ring on it." Doc's cackle sounded a lot like Marge's.

Noah came up to Bishop. "Nice turnout, right?"

"Yeah. But I don't know most of the people here."

"Cassie does. This is her town, and these are her friends, the people she serves, everyone." Noah hung an arm around his neck. "The thing is, Bish…"

"Don't call me that."

"What? It's an affectionate nickname for my future brother-in-law."

"Don't call me that."

Cassie's little brother rolled his eyes. "As I was saying, *Bishop*, in Resolute, we come together to celebrate happy times. Doesn't matter if everyone here knows everyone else. It's the spirit of the thing."

"I like that." Bishop turned Noah a bit so they had the same line of sight. "Who's he? The old, tall guy?"

"That's Charlie. He's the *last* man you want to meet."

Bishop looked at Noah in surprise. "Why's that?"

"He's the town undertaker." Noah slapped Bishop on the back and walked away laughing.

"It's time, everybody." Adam stood on a chair to get the crowd's attention. "Cassie should be here in a few minutes. Nate and Noah are going to take y'all around the far side of the house so you're ready to surprise her."

A loud buzz moved through the group as they made their way closer to the front. Bishop went to the front porch just in time to see Sean, Dave and Pete help Helen carry a gigantic cake out of her car. He held the door open for them so they could hide it inside, then joined Adam near the driveway.

"Nervous?" Adam shot him a questioning look.

"No," Bishop lied. "I'm happy." And he was.

"Good. Then you know it's right."

Bishop didn't need Adam to tell him it was right. He loved Cassie, and that love grew every single day. And Cassie's love, respect and support gave him the strength he needed to be a better man.

Cassie's SUV pulled up and stopped. Marge climbed out of the passenger seat. When Cassie's door didn't open, Marge rounded the hood and yanked it open. "You gonna just sit in there all day? Come on."

"What *is* all this?" She looked at Marge. "You said Nate called with an emergency."

"Maybe I got my messages mixed up." Marge cackled and went off to find a chair.

Bishop walked over to Cassie, took her hand and led her to the center of the dance floor.

Her head swiveled from side to side, a look of bewilderment on her face. "I don't understand."

"Remember that night at the Chute?"

That got a laugh out of her. "Not likely to forget it."

"Well, we never did get to the dancin' part of

the evening. So I figured it was about time for our first dance together."

The band, which he'd borrowed from the Chute, stood with their instruments, ready to play. But no one moved. No one spoke. Cassie looked at Bishop, her forehead creased with confusion.

He took a step back. "Sorry. I forgot something." Sliding his hand into his pocket, he came out with a small velvet box. He dropped to one knee, and Cassie's mouth dropped open. Taking advantage of her shock, he captured her hand in his. "Cassie, you've taught me that there are reasons for rules. They might not be good reasons, but they're there just the same."

The corners of Cassie's lips twitched upward.

"When I first arrived in Resolute, I thought it was you who needed to open yourself to new ideas. But I learned that I was the one with a closed mind. We've been through a lot together in a short time, and I'm hoping the adventure doesn't end anytime soon." He opened the box and held it out to her. "Will you marry me?"

Tears welled in her eyes. "Yes," she whispered.

Bishop slid the ring on her finger.

"What'd she say? I can't hear you." Marge's loud, scruffy voice blared from behind Cassie.

Cassie turned, surprise on her face once more at the sight of everyone she held near and dear venturing out from behind the house. "What in the world…"

"Are we celebrating or what?" Noah called out.

Cassie doubled over laughing.

Bishop rose and pulled a still-laughing Cassie to him. "She said yes!" he bellowed, and the whole crowd cheered.

With a radiant smile on her lips and her eyes shining with love, Cassie threw her arms around Bishop. She kissed him like he hoped he'd be kissed for the rest of his life as he danced her across the floor.

* * * * *

Get 4 FREE REWARDS!

We'll send you 2 FREE Books plus 2 FREE Mystery Gifts.

Harlequin Romantic Suspense books are heart-racing page-turners with unexpected plot twists and irresistible chemistry that will keep you guessing to the very end.

FREE Value Over $20

Get 4 FREE REWARDS!

We'll send you 2 FREE Books plus 2 FREE Mystery Gifts.

FREE Value Over **$20**

Both the **Romance** and **Suspense** collections feature compelling novels written by many of today's bestselling authors.

Get 4 FREE REWARDS!

We'll send you 2 FREE Books plus 2 FREE Mystery Gifts.

Worldwide Library books feature gripping mysteries from "whodunits" to police procedurals and courtroom dramas.

FREE
Value Over
$20